# ANGEL

A MIKE BRAVO OPS NOVELLA

EDEN FINLEY

# CHAPTER ONE_

ANGEL

IF LOOKS COULD KILL, MY MIKE BRAVO family would be dead. Not all of them, just the ones in my house. Iris, Zeus, and most of all Proxy, who brought Dipshit One and Two with him when I'd messaged an SOS.

Our boss, Trav, has implemented a rule that prevents me from killing any of them, though, so that's disappointing. Not that he had to implement that because of me or anything. He blames me, but I think it's for his own restraint more than mine. Seriously, Iris and Zeus are like the little brothers you never asked for.

Iris flops backward on my bed. "We're just saying, you looked hotter in the skirt."

"And I'm saying I didn't ask you." I glare at Proxy.

My spotter throws his hands up in defeat. "You should have said it was a fashion emergency. I thought you were in trouble."

That only makes my glare deepen. "In what world would I get myself into trouble and not be able to get out of it? You know, other than going on this blind date I let you set me up on. Why are we friends again?"

"Because you handpicked me to be your sidekick."

"And now I regret it." Not that I mean that. Proxy is my best friend in the entire world. It's just really difficult to remember that sometimes.

"Why are you so nervous?" Zeus asks. "You've had sex with a million girls."

"Not that many, thanks." And I'm nervous because I hate dating. I don't want to generalize and stereotype, but it feels like that joke about lesbians is accurate. *"What's the perfect thing to bring on a second date? A U-Haul."*

At least, that's been my experience when trying to meet someone on an app or in a bar. Meeting people in person, by chance, is impossible too. The amount of flirting I have wasted on straight women is embarrassingly high.

I'm not looking for something serious. I want consistency and dates and sex, but most of all, I want the guarantee of companionship when I'm home. I don't have the time to throw all of my energy into a relationship when I'm busy with my work. All I want is a woman who loves to have me by her side when I'm home but lets me do my thing while I'm away. The constant missed calls and messages have the potential to distract me from my life-or-death job.

I understand that I'm away a lot, and it's not like I can always keep in contact while I'm gone, but surely there's a woman out there who is as career-focused as I am, someone who will appreciate the times we can be together but throw herself into something outside of me when we're apart.

I've seen the type of relationships where couples live in each other's pockets and always want to be together—Iris and his partner, Saint, come to mind—and while that's fine ... for them, I don't think it's realistic to see that type of relationship as completely healthy or for everyone.

I'm hoping this friend of a friend of Proxy's cousin will tick all my boxes. No way in hell I'm saying that out loud with these muppets here, though. It would be nonstop jokes about my box being ticked over and over again.

Not everything is about sex. Proxy understands that being ace, but the rest of Mike Bravo? They're like horny teenagers twenty-four seven.

"Damn, Angel," Zeus says, pulling out a lingerie set from my closet and proving my point. It's made of silk and wrinkles if it's not on a hanger. It's the only reason he has a chance to see it in the first place. "You should wear this on your date."

I glance at Proxy to murder him with my gaze again, but he's already being punished enough. His face is all screwed up, and he's no doubt picturing me in said black bodysuit and garter, hooking up with another woman. The poor guy. He realized early on in his life that while he might be gay, sex is gross. His words. I happen to like sex just fine. I just don't need it like these other boneheads around me seem to.

"You know what ..." I take the lingerie from Zeus, and his eyes light up as if he, too, is picturing me the same way Proxy is. But I put it back in the closet. "Show-and-tell is over. Time to go bye-bye."

"But—" Iris goes to protest.

"Bye," I singsong.

They leave, Zeus muttering something about hoping my date is a bombshell so I'll get laid and stop being so pissy.

All the members of Mike Bravo are like my brothers, and I'm pretty sure they see me like that too. Not as their sister, but just another one of the dudes. I don't bother trying to explain the differences between men and women because, let's face it, they all think they know the answer.

PMS doesn't make me angry at them. *They* make me angry at them.

"I really am sorry," Proxy says. "I forgot your date was tonight."

Proxy would forget to show up for his own funeral if it were possible. His memory is shit.

"I just ..." I sigh. "I want to find her. The one, you know?" If the one is even a thing that exists.

"Not really because I don't have that need for someone in my life." He playfully punches my shoulder. "That's what I have you for."

"Aww, just what every lesbian needs. Her gay BFF who is sex-averse. Wow. I'm so fulfilled in the love department."

Ignoring my sarcasm, he smiles. "You're lucky to have me."

"So, so lucky." This time, even though the sarcastic tone remains, I actually mean it.

A lot of people would be happy with the kind of companionship we have. I know I'm all he needs, and if I stripped back the basic necessities of life, he and the other guys in Mike Bravo would be enough for me. But doesn't everyone want love? *Real love?*

I never bought into the Disney happily ever afters, mainly because I was confused why all the princesses wanted the prince to begin with, but I do want my happily ever after.

It might look different from what society deems as a relationship, but to have someone to come home to, to miss while I'm away, and to just know that I'm loved and cherished without the sense of clinginess … is that so much to ask?

Yes. Yes, it is too much to ask. Apparently.

I'm uncomfortable because I stupidly took Zeus and Iris's advice and wore the leather miniskirt, and we're sitting on high stools where I have to remind myself to fight the urge to sit how I normally do with my legs spread. Very unladylike. Not very demure.

Hey, all those sex ed classes about girls needing to keep their legs closed finally apply to me.

I'm also uncomfortable because my hair is down instead of in its trademark braid, and the way it tickles my neck makes me want to chop it all off. I should do it. I never wear it out, so what's the point if I'm going to spend time braiding it every day?

"Do you agree?" Lily asks, and if I'm completely honest, I have no idea what she's asking.

I tuned out about twenty minutes ago when she started talking about her five- and ten-year plans.

She's a lawyer, and with how much legal trouble Mike Bravo tends to get in, I wouldn't put it past Proxy to have set this up so we could have a direct connection to a lawyer in the future. It's the only way it would make sense. Either that or his cousin who has a friend had a friend who is a lesbian, and Proxy, dopey ace baby that he is, probably thought, "Oh, Angel is a lesbian too. That's all it takes. Let's set them up!"

"I'm sorry," I say. "What am I agreeing to?"

"That it would be better to move out of LA when it came time to having children. Maybe even California."

Somehow, I'm now having kids with this woman and moving?

I bite my lip. "Oh. Umm. Yes, I guess moving out of California to have children would make sense. If … I were at all interested in having children."

She looks confused, her brow scrunched. "What woman doesn't want children?"

Ah, this one?

"Unlike what society dictates, having children isn't always a deep-seated need in every woman's brain." Or is it their womb that is supposed to make them desire to bear children? Whatever we're "supposed" to have, I don't have it. At all.

Everyone always says I'll change my mind as I get older, but I'm approaching mid-thirties, and I still have no desire to change diapers or teach my kids that if they follow the path everyone else deems as important, life will be nothing but a disappointment.

Lily blinks at me. She has long lashes, jet-black hair like mine, but unlike my Dominican skin, she's as pale as a Stephenie Meyer vampire. Though on her, it looks good.

There's no denying that I'm attracted to her physically, but I'm sick of wasting my time when I know it's only going to end badly.

"So, you don't want kids at all, or you just don't want to be pregnant? There's always surrogacy or—"

I lean forward because something pings in my brain. "Theoretically, if we were to have kids, why wouldn't you be the one to be pregnant?"

"Oh, I wouldn't be able to take time off work. Not if I want to make partner. And if I'm on that kind of money, then I'd really need my wife to be at home with the children."

Yup. As I thought. Even though this woman is not heterosexual, she's still thinking in that heteronormative mindset. One person works, the other stays home with the children that everyone so obviously wants. Because it's not a full life unless you reproduce or some shit.

"Look," I say. "It was really nice to meet you, and I know the perfect woman is out there for you, but I'm not her. I don't want kids, and even if I did, I wouldn't want to quit my job to have them either. Just like you wouldn't. Sorry this isn't going to work."

"I understand. It sucks because, well, you're really hot, but I get it." She bites her bottom lip, and I think it's supposed to be sexy, but she has the thinnest lips of anyone I've ever seen. "I mean, we could ... while we're both single—"

"Casual never works for me," I say. Either they get too attached and think they can change me, or I keep imagining this pressure to be more than casual, which makes me lash out and do or say something stupid, like accusing them of being clingy when they're not. Yeah, it's not something I want to do again. Been there, done that, have the lipstick stains on my favorite shirts to show for it.

"Fair enough." Lily stands from her stool. "I'll probably see you around."

Considering our friend-of-a-friend connection is very loose and we've never crossed paths before, I doubt it, but I agree anyway to be polite.

She kisses me on the cheek and walks out of the now packed bar.

I'm contemplating either getting a very strong drink, banging my head on the table repeatedly, or getting out of here and ordering a very greasy, very carb-loaded pizza on the way home.

Before I can decide, an adorable, nerdy girl sits in Lily's vacated seat. She has glasses and a trendy, feminine blonde mullet, and she puts a laptop down and opens it up, burying her head into it immediately.

I don't know if she has even seen me or if she's trying to push me off my own table. "Umm, hi."

She lifts her head, and I'm struck by the pretty hazel eyes behind the thick rims of her glasses. "Oh shit, sorry. I thought you were leaving. Is anyone sitting here? There are, like, no spaces anywhere else, and I saw your friend leave ... I can go. I can—"

"No, it's okay. You can stay. I was contemplating leaving, but what can I say? I'm curious as to why someone would bring a laptop to a gay bar."

Her pretty eyes widen, and that's when I'm hit with a sense of familiarity. I know this woman from somewhere. But more importantly, that look of shock means she wasn't aware where she was. Meaning, most likely, the gorgeous nerd who I get immediate sparks with is straight.

Because that's how it always works.

She looks around the place. There's a good mix

of men, women, and enbies, so it's probably easy to look over the fact that most people are paired off or grouped with their own genders. "This is a gay bar? Huh. Didn't know that. Cool."

I cock my head. "Where do I know you fro—oh." It clicks. "You're Jamie. Harley Valentine's … assistant? Right? You're part of his entourage."

If she was shocked at learning this was a gay bar, it's nothing compared to the worry in her eyes now. In fact, it looks like I've downright terrified her.

Doing what I do best: scaring pretty women away.

# CHAPTER TWO_



PANIC CLAWS AT MY CHEST. I'VE NEVER HAD to be paranoid before, but because I've been Harley Valentine's personal assistant for over five years now, I've somehow become recognizable to people. Fans of Harley's—biggest pop star on the planet.

"Did you follow me here?" I ask.

The woman laughs, and it lights up her entire face. Honestly, she's so fucking beautiful, I don't know whether I want to be her or … I shake that thought free before I can finish it. Just like I always do when I find a woman attractive. It's an envy thing, not an attraction thing. At least, that's what my high school bestie told me when we'd kissed.

It was for a dare, and when I'd realized I wanted to actually kiss her, I stupidly told her so. "Just because we kissed, you don't have to go waving rainbow flags everywhere."

She was right, of course. Kissing someone of the same gender doesn't make you gay or automatically queer. Wanting to do it again, however … Well, I don't let myself think about that.

I'm brought back to the present by the raspy voice of the woman sitting in front of me.

"You realize you're the one who sat at my table?"

She is right. She does look familiar, but after being targeted by one of Harley's stalkers, that doesn't mean anything. She might look familiar because she has been following me, and I've seen her in passing.

"That could be a coincidence. It was the only available space," I argue, even though I saw her friend or girlfriend, whoever she was, leave.

Her lips twitch again. Apparently, I'm amusing to her. "Technically, it wasn't an available space at all. You were trying to kick me off my table."

She has this whole Michelle Rodríguez vibe, and maybe that's why I think she looks familiar. She looks like an actress.

My mouth opens to defend myself. I really did think she was leaving. But that only brings up the fact that she's right. I was the one who sat down here. Not her.

"I'm Angel," she says.

"Jamie." Oh. Right. She knows that already.

"As in Mike Bravo Angel. I worked for Harley during that stalker case a while back."

Relief and embarrassment flood through me. I remember her now. I didn't have much to do with her when she worked with Harley, but I know I met her once or twice. "I'm so sorry. I thought—" I shake my head. "Don't mind me. Ever since that guy stalked me to get to Harley, I'm paranoid of everyone. It doesn't help that I have the biggest scatterbrain to ever scatter at the moment."

"Is that why you're in a gay bar with your laptop?"

"Yes. And no. I need to work, but my boyfriend was being a dick, so I had to get out of his apartment. I'm not really familiar with this area because we just moved to this neighborhood, so I walked into the first open place I saw."

"When you say he was a dick ..."

It takes a second for me to work out what she's hinting at. "Oh! No, he didn't hurt me or anything. He's sick of how much I'm working lately, but he doesn't understand. Harley Valentine ... I love him to death. Love working for him. But he's ..."

Angel smiles again. "I remember him being pretty neurotic."

"Neurotic. Yes. Perfect word to describe him. He decided, along with his dipshit four sidekicks, to do an impromptu US tour, so I am up to my ears in schedules and hotel bookings and riders."

"Eleven are doing a reunion tour? That's amazing."

I frown at her.

"Uh, for Harley and the others in the band. Not for you. Obviously."

I shouldn't be so hard on them. I do really love my job. "I'm actually loving the work. My brain thrives on chaos. Probably because it's so chaotic up in here." I tap the side of my head. "But it's a lot. And—"

"And your boyfriend doesn't approve."

"It's not that he doesn't approve. It's just that ... he doesn't like that we don't get to spend much time together. Which is fair. But also, why does he need me to be there all. the. time? This is my dream job. Or it's at least a stepping stone to my dream job. Harley has opened so many doors and opportunities for me in the entertainment industry, and if I can pull off this last-minute tour for the most popular boy band on the planet, I could do this for real. Like, be a tour coordinator or producer. Band manager. I don't know, something bigger."

"Sounds like the boyfie has some issues with his woman being more successful than he is."

I don't want to believe that, but ever since getting more responsibility and this opportunity to prove myself, Raffy's been asking why I wasn't happy to continue to be "just Harley's PA."

"I wish I could say it was a man thing," Angel says, "but the woman you saw leaving? She's basically looking for a housewife, and she was under the assumption I make less than her."

"So my plan to break up with Raffy and become a lesbian is a bad idea?"

"Oh, so you think sexuality is a choice?"

I just about swallow my tongue. "No. Shit. Bad joke. I—"

Angel still finds me amusing. "I'm messing with you. But if you're seriously thinking about dipping your toes in the lesbian pond, there'll still be women who are the same."

"Why is it so difficult to find someone who just supports their partner? You'd think that would be base-level stuff."

"If your boyfriend doesn't support your career or what you want, I'd be reassessing that relationship if I were you."

I can't help thinking she's right. A partner should always encourage the other, support them, and yes, it sucks that we can't spend much time together right now, but I'll still be there for him when it's all said and done. It's not like I plan to run off with someone else on tour. I'll be too busy to even think about sex, let alone go out and find someone. But can I say the same about him? What will he do while I'm away if he's this mad at me and feeling lonely?

"Sorry if that depresses you. Do you want me to buy you a drink? You look like you need one."

I shake my head. "No. Thank you, though. I really do need to get this work done."

Angel glances around. "I don't think this is the place to achieve that. My house is only a few blocks away if you want to escape there until you get your work done. I've only had one drink too, so I can drive you back to your place afterward if you need it."

"That would be amazing, but I don't want to impose."

Angel slides off her stool, and my gaze catches on her long legs in her tiny skirt. She's so fucking hot that I hate her a little bit. See? It's envy. Not attraction.

"It'll probably be good for me," she says. "I want the company without the strings of expectations."

"Expectations?" I squeak.

"Yeah. Like there's zero chance of the straight girl with a boyfriend and I hooking up, so that means there'll be no wires crossed."

She's right that there's no chance of us hooking up because I won't cheat on my boyfriend, but I don't think she's right when she says there'll be no crossed wires. My wires are all over the place.

Especially when she smiles at me.

I'm so awkward as I sit on Angel's plush couch. I swear I'm fit, but her place is on a hill, and I'm sweating and panting like crazy. Her place is a nice town house, like really nice, but from what I know of Mike Bravo, they pay well.

Her home is ... weirdly feminine, with fresh flowers on her coffee table, a hanging plant out on the terrace, and potted plants in nearly every corner. I might be guilty of stereotyping her as a masc lesbian, even though she has long, silky hair, is wearing a skirt, and ... okay, so it's not so much her appearance that gives off that vibe, but I guess it's in the way she commands attention and owns a room.

I'm thankful I ran into her. I don't want to go back and face Raffy yet, plus, I can't even move until I catch my breath, so there's that. Most of all, Angel has a way about her. She has this draw that I can't shake off. Maybe there was another seat to take at that bar, but she lured me in by ... breathing.

"You okay?" she asks, holding out a glass of water for me.

I realize I'm staring and quickly glance away. "Uh, yeah. Just out of breath. I don't get to the gym as much as I should." Though I'm not sure that's the reason I can't breathe right now.

I take the water and gulp it down.

"I'm sure running after that diva boy band every day is enough cardio."

Water gets stuck in my throat as I go to laugh, and I end up choking on it. I manage to get my hand to my mouth and nose before it sprays everywhere.

Angel probably thinks I'm a huge dork, but if she does, she doesn't say it. She does smother a laugh, though. "Do you mind if I go change into my pajamas?" She plays with the waistband of her skirt that digs into her skin. She's a short woman, but I wouldn't call her petite. Her muscles have muscles. Though she doesn't have a bodybuilder physique either. Her muscles look toned and defined without being veiny. Yeah, I should tell her to cover up. I won't get any work done if I'm too busy looking at her muscles.

"Go for it. I'm the one imposing on your space here. You should be comfortable."

When she disappears from the room, I finally avert my gaze and open my laptop to get back to work. That's the reason I'm here. To work. Not to stare at the pretty woman and be an awkward little duck.

Only, when she comes back out, I can't help but stare. My fingers stop flying across the keyboard.

She's in tiny silk shorts and a matching tank top. She has a mandala tattoo up her thigh, and it disappears into the shorts. In between her cleavage, where she's so not wearing a bra, I see the tiniest bit of ink and can't help wondering if it's two different tattoos or if they link up somewhere under her clothes. She's also put her silky black hair, which almost shines deep blue, in a quick braid. Had she had her hair like that at the bar, I would've immediately recognized her.

She throws herself on the couch, and I'm saved from my trance by my phone pinging.

This goes so far past admiration for her

physique, and I probably can't ignore those *maybe I'm not so straight* thoughts anymore. Not that I need to analyze it now, having Raffy and all. Even if the thoughts of breaking up with him have been more frequent lately.

"You going to get that?" Angel asks. "Or are you ignoring it to get work done? Do you mind if I watch TV, or I can do that in my bedroom if you need silence."

All her words are a blur, but then my phone pings again. Right. Message. Phone.

I pick it up, and with only seeing the notification preview, the urge to throw my phone against the wall is so strong I would probably do it if I were anywhere else. I don't want to break Angel's things with my brick of a phone.

Angel sits up and leans forward. "That doesn't look like good news." She rests her forearms on her knees, and instead of telling her, I show her. I unlock my screen with my face and then hand it over to her to read.

I've been with Raffy since ... shit. It's been like five years now. I should be thinking about marriage with him. Children. Hell, it's taken this long for us to finally move in together. That should be a red flag, right? Five years and not even living together? And a month after moving in, it's all falling apart, and he's sending me the same recycled text he always sends when he doesn't get his own way.

We may have been together for five years, but it has been a very off-and-on five years. And every single time he does it, he hooks up with someone else and then comes crawling back to me.

"What the fuck does this mean?" Angel asks.

"It's not working. I think we should take a break. I'm going out."

I sigh. "It means we're broken up again. He'll go out, hook up, and then, like clockwork, he'll come crawling back to me saying that she didn't compare to me. He loves me. He'll never doubt that again."

Angel hands back my phone. "Until your next fight, am I right?"

"Pretty much." It sounds so manipulative now I've said it out loud.

"I'm sorry to ask this, but does he have any redeeming qualities?" Angel asks.

"Of course he does. I wouldn't be with him for five years if …" Well, shit. I trail off when I try to think of Raffy's redeeming qualities. They were abundant in the beginning. Now …

"Holy shit," I whisper. My fingers tap the screen in rapid succession.

"What is it?"

"I've realized something. I'm not happy in my relationship anymore."

Out of the corner of my eye, I see Angel's lips purse, but I'm too busy typing out a long response to acknowledge her judgment.

*You're right. We should take a break. An extended one. Like, forever. I haven't been happy for a long time, and all you do is try to manipulate me into giving up my job, my friends, my everything so I can be with you. I can no longer put you first. I'm going to be my first and only priority from now on. We're over. For good this time.*

I hit Send and smile, feeling lighter than I have in years even if it does mean I now have to move out of the apartment I just moved into with him. With any luck, he'll be the one to move out. I can afford the rent on my own. I'm not so sure he could. Eh, future Jamie's problem to work out.

"What did you say?" Angel asks.

"Just that we're over for good this time."

"Are you, though?"

I fucking hate that the little voice in the back of my mind says "No" while my mouth says "Yes."

# CHAPTER THREE_
## ANGEL

Jamie looks like she's about to cry, and I am so not equipped to deal with that. It's not that I'm an emotionless robot, but emotions make me uncomfortable. Especially relationship emotions, because I'm not sure I've ever had a genuine relationship to know what it's like to love someone so fiercely. I've definitely never been with someone for *five years*. I almost fell off the couch when Jamie said how long they'd been together. My record is ten times shorter than that. Six months is usually where I decide if I want to go all in, and in those six months, each and every partner has shown me why they're not the woman for me.

"Do you want a drink?" I ask. "Wine? I have some red wine somewhere."

Jamie sniffs and refuses to lift her head. Her laptop is still on her lap, open, but the screen has gone to sleep because all she's doing is staring at her phone. "Got anything stronger?"

"Tequila?"

"Perfect."

Filling that request will probably result in tonight getting messy, but if it stops her from crying, it'll be worth it. Messy, I can deal with. Tears? I'd rather wear electrified nipple clamps. Not to be dramatic or anything.

I pull down the tequila and some shot glasses from the cabinet above my fridge and place them on the coffee table. "Are you sure you want to do this? I feel like I should be the responsible one here and at least point out that it's a bad idea."

"Worse than spending five years with someone and being broken up with via text?"

"Enough said." I slink to the floor, pour two shots, and hand her one.

She downs it and holds out the empty glass for more, so instead of drinking mine, I give it to her.

She screws up her face this time, and the scrunch in her nose is all kinds of adorable. "Again."

I take her glass but set it on the coffee table. "How about we wait until those two kick in first."

"Fine." Jamie closes her laptop and puts it on the couch beside her before slinking back into the cushions. "Why did it take me so long to figure out Raffy wasn't who I thought he was?"

"Because you love him. I'm guessing." Ugh, that makes me want a tequila. I refill one of the glasses and throw it back.

What even is love?

I know I love Proxy and my Mike Bravo family, even if they piss me off a lot of the time, but real romantic love? I'm not sure I'm capable of it because I will always put myself first, and apparently, that's not how relationships work.

"I thought I loved him," Jamie says quietly. "I

mean, you have to love someone to be with them for five years, right? Or to keep taking them back after they use loopholes to cheat on you?"

"I'm the wrong person to ask that."

"Why?"

"I was just thinking to myself that I don't even know what love is. If I were in your position, I would've left the first time my partner cheated."

"Technically, we were on a br—"

"Let's not get all Ross and Rachel on this."

Jamie cocks her head. "Who?"

"Ouch. Way to make me feel old. How old are you, anyway?"

"Twenty-six."

"Oh, so you're a fetus. Got it." But I mean, seven years isn't that much of a difference.

"Fetus? What does that make you? A newborn? You can't be that much older than me. You don't look a day over thirty."

I mock gasp. "I'm twenty-nine."

Jamie's eyes widen to the point she looks like an anime character. "Can I have that next shot? I need to bury my embarrassment in a bottle of tequila."

"Sounds healthy." Yet, I pour her another one anyway and hand it over. "By the way, I'm actually thirty-four."

She huffs and downs the shot, wincing as she says, "I don't know how to take you."

"You and most of the world. Sorry if I'm crossing a line. Mike Bravo's love language is insults and teasing, so I sometimes forget not everyone can tell when I'm joking."

"It doesn't help that you're extremely intimidating."

On anyone else, I would assume that was flirting. Jamie blinks at me, and unlike when Lily bit her lip earlier, when Jamie does it now, it only emphasizes how full and plump her lips are.

"I'm really not that intimidating," I say.

"I disagree. You look like a goddess, your body is amazing, and you're so freaking pretty it hurts to look at you."

"And I think three tequilas is your limit." Also, this is why lesbians have a hard time meeting women. Because when you have a woman complimenting you like that, it's easy to mistake it for flirting when it's actually someone just complimenting someone else.

I need another tequila.

Mid-pour, however, Jamie says, "We should hook up," and it takes me so much by surprise that I accidentally knock the bottle of Patrón against the shot glass.

It topples over, I drop the bottle, and then my very tasty, very expensive tequila is all over the coffee table and carpet.

Jamie jumps off the couch. "Shit, sorry, I didn't mean—uh … where's a towel to clean this up?"

I'm too busy staring at my carpet and wondering if I suck the tequila out of it that it will be too much on the nose. The carpet-munching jokes would write themselves.

But that's not really the thing I'm stuck on. It's what I'm forcing myself to focus on because of what she said.

If it was a joke, it's kinda mean. If it was for real

…

While I've been sitting here on the floor, Jamie found my paper towels in the kitchen. She appears in front of me and then drops to her knees, wiping the coffee table down and then pressing paper towel into the carpet to soak up the mess.

But I can't stop staring at her. At her pouty lips. Her soft eyes and the way her fake lashes frame them perfectly.

"Did you mean it?" I ask.

She hangs her head. "I did in the moment, but now I realize how I shouldn't put you in that position."

"Which position is that, exactly?"

"The one where I'd just be using you."

It's like a gut punch. "To get back at your ex?"

"Well, that, but also … more than just that …" There she goes biting that lip again. When she talks, it all comes out in a rush. "I kissed my friend in high school and wanted more but was told that doesn't mean I'm queer, and tonight … well, tonight … you … and …"

My lips twitch. So maybe it was flirting after all.

I lean forward, and she freezes. She's practically hovering above me because she's on her knees in front of me, and I'm on my ass, but she's turned into a statue, so I pause. "I have to say, hooking up to get back at an ex is petty, but you wanting me because you're confused is something I can get on board with."

Her hazel eyes flick to mine, those long lashes batting at me. "It-it is?"

I nod. "If you want to. No pressure from me."

She averts her gaze again and says, "Okay."

She seems so sure about it too.

I force a laugh and pull away. "You seem unsure now."

"No, no, I'm not. I mean, I am. Sure. I'm not

unsure. I just … I was expecting you to tell me I'm not … not …"

"Not, what? Attractive? Have you seen you?"

Her cheeks pinken at that. "No, that I'm not queer enough or whatever. Or I don't know what I'm doing. Or I've had three tequila shots and am not thinking clearly. And I mean, why would you choose to hook up with someone with no experience, who might be tipsy, just broke up with her boyfriend, and—"

"Wow. You're really selling me on this."

Jamie sighs and then lands on her ass next to me. "I'm a mess."

"You are. But you're a cute mess if that helps at all."

"Not really. I'd rather be a sexy mess." She manages a small smile.

"Well, you're that too, but I more meant how nervous you are about me. And while I don't like that you expected me to pull the gold-star lesbian card, I can acknowledge that's not about me. Someone must have been really fucking cruel to you for you to think that way."

Jamie nods. "The thing is, working for Eleven, I'm around gay and queer guys a lot. So I understand the struggle, especially with Harley and how difficult it was for him to come out to the public. But yeah, my only experience was that crush I had on my best friend in high school, and because of her and some others saying I only wanted to kiss her for attention, I guess …"

"You protected yourself by believing and agreeing with them?"

She nods again.

"That's total bullshit. I find whenever someone's experience doesn't match their own, they think everyone else's is somehow wrong or not accurate. Everyone's journey and feelings are different, and that's what I actually love about being part of the queer community. You just have to find the right people to help you navigate it."

"A-and a-are you that person?"

I press my lips together. The last thing I need is to experiment with a straight girl and have her become clingy or obsessive. I don't usually like casual hookups either. But with Jamie ... there's something about her that just draws me in. "I could be."

Jamie's breath hitches.

"But I'd want you to be sure," I say before I let her get ahead of herself. "Maybe you should make sure you're properly broken up with your boyfriend before making any rash decisions."

"I'm done with him." It's the most confident she has sounded in the last ten minutes.

"You're still angry. Why don't you wait until tomorrow? You're welcome to stay the night here."

The hopeful look on her face is almost too difficult to kill.

"On the couch."

Her shoulders sag, but she only lets it show for a second before she straightens back up.. "You're right. I should ... wait. The tequila doesn't want me to, but it does make sense."

"I'm going to go to bed. You're welcome to stay up and work for as long as you need. I'll get you a blanket and pillow for when you get tired."

"Thank you for doing this. Seriously."

I stand. "It's no problem."

I get the blanket and pillow, say good night, and I just know that I'll be dreaming of those red lips. I wish I'd kissed her instead of bringing up all the valid points of why kissing her is a bad idea. But I know that if I was meant to kiss her, she'll still be there in the morning. Sober. Wanting to still hook up.

Yet, when morning comes, I walk out of my bedroom and into an empty living room. The blanket and pillow I gave her are folded neatly, and there's a note written on some paper towel, sitting on top.

*Thank you for talking me down last night. I appreciate it. Maybe I'll see you around sometime.*

There's a poorly drawn winky face after that. Or maybe it's a smiley face? It's hard to tell.

It's also hard to tell the tone of that note. Is she thanking me for actually talking her down last night, or does she mean she's thankful I didn't let us hook up?

If that's the case, it's best that we didn't.

Even if I was really looking forward to it.

# CHAPTER FOUR_

JAMIE

Brix, Harley's live-in head of security and boyfriend, puts the last box of my stuff in my new room.

"Thank you, guys, for letting me stay here until I can get a new lease on an apartment." I felt terrible having to ask my boss to let me live with him, but like he put it, none of us will be here soon, as we'll all be out on tour, so really, it's as if I'm just using one of many rooms in Harley's mansion as storage.

But also, I get the feeling Harley likes having me around. My worry is that means if he needs anything, instead of texting me, he'll come to my room instead. Don't sane and rational people choose not to live at their workplace for this very reason?

I can't escape.

Harley puts his arm around my shoulders. "Now that you're all moved in, how about you fetch me some coffee?"

Brix grunts. "I told you those kinds of jokes won't be appreciated, yet you said it anyway."

Harley saunters over to his boyfriend and looks up at him with the most innocent expression he can muster. And being in a boy band, even if he's now in his thirties, he can still pull off that pouty look. "It's because I have you, my big, strong protector, to hold her at bay when she comes at me with a knife."

I can't help laughing at my boss, who is more friend than employer. "I'll go make coffee. You want one, Brix?"

He looks torn, and Harley mocks him for it.

"Ooh, ethical dilemma. Will you let my personal assistant get you coffee after your big stand just now?"

"It's the least I could do," I say. "You did move all my boxes from Raffy's apartment."

And it did become Raffy's apartment. It's been a week since the night we broke up, six days since he tried to win me back after admitting he hooked up with someone that night. It was the same recycled story, and thanks to Angel, I had the clear mind to tell him to fuck off. My only regret was not hooking up with her so I could throw that in his face.

Harley scoffs. "Raffy. I told you not to date a guy with a dog's name, but you never listen to me."

"Well, if you had told me that he was a slimeball instead, maybe I would have listened. Your entire dislike for him was because of a name his parents gave him and was something he had no choice in the matter."

"Are you saying his name wasn't actually

Rafael? Or Rafe? His parents actually named him Raffy?"

I throw my hands up. "You're a celebrity. You should be used to meeting kids with unusual names."

I turn and head down the hall toward the kitchen to make the coffee. I'm going to make Brix's extra strong because I have something to ask him. I'm in need of his … contacts.

I'm putting on the finishing touches—a leaf design in Harley's latte, and, well, Brix drinks his black enough to be confused with battery acid, so that one is simple—when both Harley and Brix join me.

"Just in time," I say and hand over their drinks. "Also, while I have you, I had an idea for the tour."

"I'm listening," Harley says, but it's not him I'm talking to.

"Actually, it had to do with security." I glance at Brix.

"What about it? We have it covered."

"Yeah, with venue security. I was just thinking that it's such a short tour, and there's so many moving parts. With the guys' partners coming with us, like Jordan and Lyric, and even Maggie and the kids, because Ryder tells me he will not be going on tour without his kids or their mother, even if Maggie is kicking and screaming about being dragged on a groupie tour—"

"Jamie, you're getting sidetracked and rambly," Harley points out.

"Right. Sorry. I was thinking it wouldn't be a horrible idea to hire bodyguards for all of us. Not only for venue protection. And I figured your old company Mike Bravo would be good to handle that, right?"

Brix rubs his chin. "It's not a terrible idea to have extra security around."

Harley folds his arms. "Do we get a say in it? You know Mason will hate it. So will Maggie. She doesn't even want to be on the tour, and now you're saying she'll have someone tailing her? The ex-army soldier who could handle herself?"

"I'll contact Mike Bravo today," Brix says and walks away.

Harley holds out his arms. "Am I invisible?"

Brix calls back at the same time I speak, and we both say, "Yes."

Now to somehow make Mike Bravo choose Angel to send on this tour.

Sure, I could ask Brix for her number, but considering I have no idea where my head is at with all this *I'm going through a breakup and am not so straight* stuff, I don't want to have to explain it when I don't have answers myself.

All I know is that ever since leaving her house that morning, I haven't stopped thinking about the way she leaned in closer to me.

I was sure she was about to kiss me, and I froze, even though everything inside me was screaming to close the gap. To see if her lips were as soft as they looked, if her hands were as strong as I imagined, and to find out once and for all if my desire to kiss my best friend in high school was a fleeting thing or if I really am bi. Or pan. Or fluid. Whatever I might be.

I hope I get my chance with Angel to figure it out.

Having the job that I do, I've met celebrities. A lot. Everyone from the current superstars hitting the charts, to one-hit wonders, to the legends that fill the entertainment industry. But I've never been as nervous meeting any celebrity as I am right now, waiting for the Mike Bravo hires to show up to go through their duties next week when we leave for the tour.

It's been a month since I've seen Angel, and as I stare at the contracts and NDAs on the coffee table in Harley's living room, I'm tempted to move the little Post-it with Angel's name on it.

So what if I kind of manipulated the situation so she would be my bodyguard? Is this how I flirt now? Just straight up forcing her to spend time with me? Is that, like, considered kidnapping?

Maybe I should swap her name with Domino's. As the only straight man on the Mike Bravo roster, he's been assigned to babysit Maggie and her two kids, whom she shares with Ryder and Lyric. It was those two knuckleheads' request, and I don't think they know how much trouble they're going to be in when Maggie finds out what they did.

I love Maggie, but she's scary. Not in the way Angel is scary, but mom energy scary. Angel is ... intimidating scary. Intimidatingly hot.

It turns out her nickname isn't because she looks like a fallen angel, all gorgeous with her golden skin and long jet-black hair. And there I go, picturing her again. In her little silky sleep shorts. I swear, I look back on that night and see her with this ethereal glow around her that I've obviously made up in my mind, but my point is, in the month since staying at her house, I haven't been able to stop thinking about her.

So finding out her nickname is actually Angel of Death because she's a sniper—something I didn't know until Brix told me—should have been the moment I hesitated or got scared. But if anything, it only made me more interested in her.

Hello, therapy? I might need your help.

Now that this is happening, though, now that my plan to assign her as my bodyguard is coming to fruition, I'm wondering if I should chicken out. Forcing someone to spend time with me is not the way to get them to date me. But getting her contact information from Brix and being up-front about it is way too forward for me.

How does a baby bisexual get queer people interested?

I was kind of hoping Angel would reach out to me, but I understand why she didn't. She doesn't know whether I went home and made up with Raffy or was drunk and can't remember throwing myself at her. I definitely remember that embarrassment, but I also can't hate the moment all that much.

Because she not only made me realize that I deserve better than Raffy, but she also made me face those niggly feelings I've had since high school. It turns out they were real and that I should have believed in myself and my own feelings. I should have ignored it when others told me how I was feeling.

There's no doubt I'm attracted to Angel. And that's why I'm still staring at her Post-it, telling myself to leave it when my nerves really want me to switch it.

This plan was a good one until now, when I actually have to face her.

Brix enters the house with his old teammates in tow, and the noise of the front door opening and voices filtering down the hallway makes me jump a mile high. Too late to chicken out now.

I leave the seating area I've set up for them and welcome them as they come inside the house.

Angel is the third person to walk through the front door, and I swear, watching her and the other Mike Bravo people is like one of those action movies where all the attractive people walk in slow motion.

My face suddenly feels hot, and I try to avoid looking at her directly like she's the sun or some shit. It lasts maybe two seconds.

Angel's cut off her long hair in the last month and now sports a lopsided bob with an undercut on one side.

I thought she was gorgeous before. Now, she's . . .

I swallow hard and force my professional smile. Because I have to be professional—ignoring the fact that I got her here in a nonprofessional manner.

"Welcome," I croak. *Great start, Jamie.* "If you'll follow me, I have all your paperwork lined up."

It takes everything inside me not to dive at them and finally make the Post-it switch. That would be too obvious.

I bite my bottom lip and risk another glance in Angel's direction. Yep, definitely couldn't pull it off now with her staring at me.

"Your assignment brief and NDAs to sign are in your employment packets." I gesture to the table where they are, and they each grab theirs and take a seat.

I can't help watching Angel as she picks up her folder and opens it up because I know what she's seeing. *I'm her assignment.*

Will she run? Ask to swap with someone else? I'm too scared to find out, so I hold my breath like that will delay this moment.

Instead of doing either of those things, her lips quirk, and her deep brown eyes meet mine. Butterflies erupt in my stomach.

I try for an innocent smile, but I'm scared it comes out as psychotic more than anything. I'm sure it's not helping me look like less of a stalker. I might as well club her over the back of her head while I'm at it.

# CHAPTER FIVE_

ANGEL

BRIX GOES THROUGH OUR DUTIES AND responsibilities, and while technically, he will be protecting Harley, I'm assigned to his ... team. Meaning, somehow, coincidentally, I'm in charge of Jamie's safety.

It's only been a month, but somehow, she looks younger. Like she's had a chemical peel or Botox or something. This is Hollywood. It's possible.

That only makes me think of her lips. How plump they are. How I almost got the chance to feel them against mine. Are they made of filler? Would that make them soft or hard?

I really hope Brix isn't telling us important stuff right now because I'm not listening. Before I know it, the meeting wraps up, and we're being told to go meet with our assignments. Another coincidence that mine is in this very room?

I take my chance to talk to her while the others are all distracted briefly catching up with Brix before they go on their merry way to the other boy band members' houses.

Jamie watches me as I approach her, but the closer I get, the more her attention diverts to different spots of the room. She's still as cute as the night we met in the bar, her thick rims hiding her shiny hazel eyes. This time, she's the one in the skirt, though hers is professional knee-length, but even so, my gaze is drawn to her legs. Never thought I was a legs kind of woman, but there's something about the way hers look while wearing ankle-high red stripy heels that has me questioning if I can stay professional on this job.

It takes a billion years for me to cross the room and get to her, but as soon as I do, those pretty eyes flicker to mine.

"Y-you cut your hair."

I can't hide my grin. "It's nice to see you again too. Hello. How are you?"

I was hoping I'd get to see her blush again, and it's taken me less than ten seconds to do it.

"Right. Sorry. Hi."

"Being single looks good on you," I say. "Unless you've been making weekly appointments with Harley's cosmetic surgeon."

She frowns. "You know I'm single?"

Ope. She caught me there. "I ... might have asked around about you."

"But you never called me?" Jamie cocks her head.

"Not really my style."

"Calling people?"

I snort. "Well, that too, but I meant chasing after straight girls because they drunkenly showed me attention. I'd rather wait until they convince their boss to hire me as their bodyguard before making my move."

Jamie tries to hide her smile. "Smooth move, but how do you know that's what happened here? Maybe this is all a coincidence and I'm not a crazy stalker person who convinced their boss to hire extra security when we probably don't need it."

"If that's the case, then obviously fate wanted us to meet again. Though, I have to say, crazy stalker Jamie sounds more fun than leaving it up to the universe."

Her plump lips flatten. "Well, now I don't know whether I should admit to it or not."

I laugh. "You don't have to admit anything. I know all your secrets. Right down to the time you got six parking tickets in one week while on jury duty when you were eighteen."

"They didn't have it clearly marked," she argues. "How was I supposed to know you're not allowed to park in front of a fire hydrant?"

Young, naive Jamie is cute too.

"I mean, I know that now, but if you ask me, it's rude that they make you do jury duty and then don't supply parking for it." She finally pauses. "Wait, how did you know—"

I lean in close to her and whisper, "You're not the only one who has stalker tendencies. Plus, I have easy access to background checks."

"After everything I've been through, that should probably scare me."

She's right about that. We probably shouldn't be making jokes about stalkers when she had one a few years ago. But the way she said she *should* be scared … "Does it scare you?"

"Nowhere near as much as it should."

Right answer. "Sounds like this tour is going to be fun."

"It will be. You know how when you go to a concert and the band always plays a new song from their new track that you've never heard so you can't sing at the top of your lungs? The guys didn't do that this time. It's all the classics. It'll be amazing."

I smile. "Jamie, I wasn't talking about the concerts."

And there I go, making those cheeks pinken again.

▭

As a bodyguard, my job is to shadow Jamie but stay invisible. That's really fucking impossible when she doesn't stop moving. It's like she runs on never-ending batteries. She really wasn't joking when she said she thrives on chaos.

While it's easy for me to keep up with her, I don't know if I could do it wearing the heels she does.

The most I step outside my combat boots is a knee-high boot with little height. I'll wear heels if I need to on a job, so I can walk in them if I have to. I just don't want to. I'm convinced stilettos were invented by men for the sole purpose of not letting women run away from them.

But Jamie could be like that redhead in *Jurassic World* and run away from a T-Rex in hers. If there's something I'm a sucker for more than a hot, nerdy girl, it's competency. And watching Jamie tackle any and all situations that come her way definitely makes me take notice.

It's the first show of the tour, so there's bound

to be teething problems, but she handles every-thing like a pro. She doesn't fluster once.

Which makes me question if it's a me-specific thing or a social stutter she has.

It's not until halfway through the concert that she finally gets a chance to hang backstage and watch Eleven's set.

The stage lights paint her face in blue and purple hues, and while she focuses on the guys, her lips moving along to every line of the songs, I'm only focused on her.

She's wearing contacts tonight, so she's missing the frames I like so much, but without them, her hazel eyes are free to shine. They practically dance with the reflection of the stage lights, and as she watches Eleven's set, she has this glow about her. Like she literally radiates happiness.

I'd hate her if I wasn't so damn attracted to her.

The concert winds down, and then we're on the move again. If we were cartoon characters, steam would be coming from her heels.

I've been in war zones. I've shot people down, taken them out from over a mile away, and I've done shit no regular citizen could ever do. But this type of work? I couldn't do it. No way.

Jamie is something special, and she deserves to know that. I'm assuming the ass of a boyfriend she had a month ago didn't tell her. Not once.

So when she's finally done for the night, staying back way longer than anyone else in the venue, I don't even fight the urge to tell her.

We arrive at her hotel room door—we're a full-service company here at Mike Bravo, from sunup to end of day, we don't leave our charges' sides—and she does that awkward end of date thing. She stops walking and fishes out her key card to swipe into the room, but she doesn't put it to the little key fob reader. She also doesn't say anything.

It looks like she wants to, but her mouth isn't cooperating.

So I talk for her. "You looked really good out there tonight. You were in your element."

"It could have run smoother. I'll have all those kinks ironed out by the next one."

"I don't think the crowd realizes how many working parts there are to put on a concert like this. It was an experience for me, that's for sure. I wish I could say I wasn't an Eleven fan back in the day, but what else was I supposed to listen to when I was a teenage lesbian trying to stay in the closet? You did an amazing job, and I'm kinda in awe of you."

Instead of maybe blushing again or going shy, Jamie holds her head high. "Thank you. But I will get those little blips ironed out."

I love her tenacity and confidence when it comes to this stuff, yet when I risk putting my hand on her shoulder and she practically melts under my touch, I love that I can make her frazzled.

It's one hand, a minor touch, but her reaction sends a thrill right through me that's addictive. "You're where you belong, Jamie. And no one, no boyfriend, no partner, not anybody should tell you any different."

"I'll never believe in anyone else more than I believe in myself from now on."

"Good. At least one good thing came from breaking up with that douchebag."

Jamie smiles. "I can think of another."

"Yeah?"

The subtle nod, the small lick of her lips ... I really hope this is going where I think it is.

"It means I'm free to do this." Jamie steps forward, pressing against me. She's the one making the first move, and though I like her bashful side, I might love this more.

Her mouth collides with mine, hard at first, and then soft. Jamie's lips taste like bubble gum lip gloss, even if she hasn't reapplied it in the last hour or so. I haven't been timing it or anything, but I do remember watching her do it. I couldn't look away.

Kissing Jamie is better than I could have imagined. Her confidence sticks around, and I open my mouth for her when her tongue presses against my lips. I let her tongue in, stroking it with mine, and when she lets out a moan, I can't help myself.

I turn us and push her back against her hotel door. Jamie clings to my leather jacket, as if she's trying to pull me closer, but I'm flush with her amazing body.

With her heels, we're about the same height, and even though we're in public, I can't help pushing my leg in between hers.

She immediately grinds against it, not even caring that anyone could walk by at any second.

She fumbles around for the key card she pulled out earlier—I have no idea where it went, and it's obvious neither does she—but we don't stop kissing.

Jamie's free hand works its way to the side of my head that's been recently shaved, and as her fingers glide over the short hair, it sends shivers down my spine.

I really want her to find that key. I want to follow her into her hotel room, undress her, and have some fun exploring each other, but this tour is six weeks long. We're at the beginning of this thing, and the last thing I want to do is hook up and have her regret it.

She finally pulls her mouth away from mine, and she takes a gasping breath. "We should take this inside."

I smile. "We should. But I'm only going to agree if you're sure."

Those long, fake lashes blink up at me. "I'm sure. What if there's some fanboy or girl in there waiting to shiv me?"

I laugh. "When it comes to pickup lines, I have to say, that's a pretty good one."

"So, will you?" Her hazel eyes almost make it impossible to say no. "Come inside, I mean."

"I'm ... contemplating."

"Contemplating what?"

"If you'll regret it tomorrow, and then we'll have to spend the next six weeks together."

Jamie steps away from me but is dead serious when she says, "The only thing I regret in the last six weeks is not doing this from the start."

Well, now, how am I supposed to say no to that?

# CHAPTER SIX_

JAMIE

I MAY BE FAKING CONFIDENCE LIKE A PRO—the whole entertainment industry is full of that "fake it until you make it" attitude—but as Angel pulls me inside my hotel room, I'm too nervous and way too into Angel to make the next move. I don't know where to start.

"Change your mind?" Angel asks with a knowing twitch of her lips.

"Not at all. I'm just … nervous."

"You don't need to be. If I do anything you're uncomfortable with—"

"Oh, I'm not nervous about what you will do. Do whatever you want to me."

Angel grins. "So you're nervous about what you'll do to me?"

"I'm nervous if I'll do it *well*."

She reaches for me, cupping the side of my face. Her touch is soft, but the calluses from years of military training and ops are rough against my skin. "You don't need to worry about that."

"Why not?"

"That's all part of the fun. Figuring each other out. Exploring. Sex is supposed to be fun, Jamie. Not nerve-racking."

She's right, I know she is, but I guess … "Is it weird I've never really thought about being able to get a guy off? They just usually take what they need."

Angel screws up her face. "Thank fuck I'm gay."

She's making this easier on me by taking the seriousness out of the moment.

"It's … it's a lot of pressure. That's all."

"Think about how I feel. You might be so disappointed by girl-on-girl action that I ruin you for all other women. I don't want to force you to have to have sex with men for the rest of your life. I couldn't live with that kind of guilt."

I laugh. "Well, when you put it like that."

"Why don't we take it one step at a time?"

"O-one step at a time," I repeat.

But what the fuck is the first step?

I don't know what I was expecting with a woman like Angel. Possibly that because she's on the more masculine side of the coin, she would somehow behave like a man would, but that thought is only reiterating the harmful stereotypes that had my friend tell me once that I'm not queer just because we kissed.

Only I get to decide what label I am, and as I stand across from Angel, nervous as fuck but so ready for more with her, the bisexual label finally feels fitting. Like I'm not some imposter or wannabe.

Should I have needed to experience this with Angel to get to the point where a label felt right?

No. But that's what happens when you listen to others instead of what's inside.

Angel smiles and takes off her leather jacket. She's only in a crop top and her tight black pants and boots, but somehow, I think she looks hotter now than if she were to take the rest of her clothes off.

The tattoo down the side of her torso, the way her ring finger, pinky, and thumb don chunky jewelry on each hand, and how her new haircut sits just right, framing one side of her face … she doesn't need to be naked to be intimidatingly attractive.

She reaches her hand out and pulls me toward her. "Come here."

I go willingly and let her lead me toward the hotel bed.

"One step at a time," she reminds me, and then she leans in.

I suck in a sharp breath as she keeps closing the gap between us. We must be a million miles apart because it takes forever for her lips to find mine. But when that does inevitably happen, I wrap my arms around her back and hold on while she kisses me senseless. Literally. Sounds, light, all distractions fade away.

All I can feel is the heat of her skin. All I can taste is the sweetness of her lips.

And when she pushes me down on the bed and climbs on top of me, that feeling of drowning in her only intensifies.

One gentle hand skirts up my neck, while her other hand slips under my skirt and grips my outer thigh.

My hips thrust upward, trying to get her hand higher. My hands tremble, unsure of what to do.

Angel doesn't hesitate. Her touch is confident. Strong, yet soft.

I want to touch her too, but it's impossible to know where to start. I could go north, south … anywhere in between. Between is good. Safe. Not intimidating.

Okay, it's still a little intimidating. I practically punch her in the stomach while trying to make my move.

She breaks from my mouth and lets out a huffy laugh.

"Fuck. Sorry." This is going so well. *Good job, Jamie.*

Angel laughs some more, and the sound eases some of the tension in my gut.

She lifts up to rest on her elbows so she can stare down at me. "Still nervous?"

"What gave it away?" I say dryly.

"We're going slow, remember? You can touch me anywhere you want. You don't have to rush it."

Even though I nod, my eyes must give me away.

"Or we can stop right here—"

"No," I'm quick to say. "But I … and I want …"

"Tell me what you want."

"Everything. Nothing. To just get over this nervousness. I feel like I'm a virgin again."

"If you really want to keep going, I can take the lead. Do everything for us."

Okay, this time, I can tell my eyes widen.

"Don't worry. I won't be breaking out the advanced moves. If you enjoy tonight, maybe we can pull those out next time. If there is a next time."

I definitely want there to be a next time, but

maybe I should wait to see if I die of embarrassment from this encounter first. "I want you to take the lead. Touch me." My voice comes out in a rasp and an octave lower than usual. "Please touch me."

Instead of doing as I ask, she pulls up completely and stands. My skirt is halfway up my thighs, and I'm sure I'm on full display, but I don't care, especially as her gaze roams over me while she strips out of her tight black pants, revealing lacy boy short underwear.

My mouth waters, and I want her body heat back on mine.

I don't have to wait long. She climbs back on top of me, straddling my legs this time.

Both her hands creep their way from my hips up my sides to my shoulders and then down my arms. Shivers tingle my spine. Goose bumps break out on my skin. She interlinks our fingers together and leans down and goes back to kissing me.

I get so lost in her mouth, her tongue, that when she pins my arms above my head, I don't know how they got there.

My face heats, and my hips do that lifting thing again. I want friction. She still hasn't touched me where I want her to, and I'm dying.

Angel shifts so she's pinning my hands with only one of hers now. She's not gripping tight, but I'm not going to move anyway. Here is good. There's no pressure on where to put my hands or what to do. From this position, all I have to do is feel.

And the second she gives me what I want, that contact and friction between my legs, I've never almost come so fast. Tingles, heat, and all-over want take over.

Her thumb brushes over my clit through my panties, moving over it with such precision I can't understand how men can't find it.

I wince at my own thoughts and tell myself to not compare. This isn't about comparing. This is about experiencing something I should've let myself do a long time ago. And so far, it's ten out of ten. Highly recommend.

I moan into Angel's mouth, and she takes that as an invitation to take the next step. She can take the whole staircase for all I care. Go all the way. Because as she lifts the hem of my panties and slips her fingers inside the material, I gasp, my lips breaking from hers. She hasn't even touched me anywhere yet.

She teases me, her thumb still working me over my underwear and her middle finger circling my entrance. I want her to push it inside me.

When she does, all self-consciousness goes out the window. Angel kisses my neck as I throw my head back and writhe beneath her, wanting more.

Her breathing gets heavy, and that's when my attention draws toward her hips moving as fiercely as mine. While she works me over, she uses that same hand to grind against.

I'm still fully dressed, and I have no fucking clue how she can get me so close so fucking easily. I don't think I've come from someone using their fingers since maybe high school. It's almost as if once you have full penetrative sex in the hetero world, there's no going back to the basics.

This might be basic, but holy fucking shit, it's so extra. It's so fucking good.

There's only one more thing I need to send me over the edge. Her thumb making circles, driving me higher and higher ... I need it just a bit harder. I lift my hips again and hold firm, my ass off the mattress. My body tightens around her finger, my whole body flushes, and when she adds a second finger inside me, that's what sets me off.

I let out a string of curses, followed by begging. "Kiss me." I let out a hard breath. "Kiss me," I say again. Like it's the only thing I'm able to say until she does it.

In the next second, I can taste her lips again and feel her tongue in my mouth. My muscles uncoil, and I sink back onto the mattress. She removes her hand from between us and lowers her weight on top of me. All the while, our mouths never separate.

It's not until I catch my breath and come back down to earth that I realize I don't know if she found that as explosive as I did.

I pull back. "Wait, did you—"

She smiles. "I had that covered. Don't you worry."

"But I should because, I mean, I can't tell, and ... oh my God ..." I flop backward into the pillow. "This is how all the guys I've been with have felt. How the hell are you supposed to know if there's no ... substance?"

Angel rolls off me, laughing breathlessly. "Substance?"

"I couldn't think of a less cringey word than cum."

She glances over at me, smile not leaving her face. "I want you to feel something. Are you okay with me guiding your hand?"

I roll onto my side and reach for her, and as she moves my hand into her underwear, I can feel exactly how turned on that made her. She's wet, her underwear as well.

"This is what you do to me," she whispers. Then she presses one of her fingers inside her, along with one of mine.

My heart is in my throat as she guides me. Her body is tight and warm around my finger, and I want to keep going.

So when Angel asks if I'll be okay to keep going if she removes her hand, all I do is nod and take over.

She tells me what to do. "Deeper." "Another finger." "Rub the heel of your hand against my clit."

This time when she comes, I don't miss it. It's impossible to. Her eyes roll back in her head, her lips part, and the husky moan she lets out leaves no doubt in my mind.

I don't know if I trust that she came the first time, and that's just something I'm going to have to accept, but this makes me feel a hell of a lot better.

The only question I have left is ... "What happens now?"

"I don't know about you, but orgasms knock me out."

Orgasms. Plural. Go me!

"I can stay or go back to my room," Angel says. "Up to you."

I try not to smile. "What if someone tries to break into my hotel room?"

"Shit. I'd be the worst bodyguard in the world if I wasn't here for that."

"Guess that means you have to stay." And damn, isn't that a shame.

# CHAPTER SEVEN_

ANGEL

I'M AWOKEN BY NEARBY VOICES, BUT THEY
sound like they're talking through a wall. It takes a
couple of seconds to get my bearings, to remember
I'm in Jamie's hotel room, and that the empty spot
beside me means she's already up. Working or
having a straight-girl freak-out, I'm not entirely
sure yet.

Last night was fun.

I'm not usually one for needing reassurance or
promises the morning after sleeping with someone,
but considering we're still going to be working together for the next five weeks, I need to know she's
at least okay.

I roll over and see she's half out the door to the
hotel room, keeping the gap so small that whoever
she's talking to wouldn't be able to see in.

First sign things might not be okay if she
doesn't want anyone to know I spent the night.

All right. Damage control.

I climb out of bed and find my pants on the
floor. Now that I'm up, I can hear it's Brix and

Harley Jamie's talking to. Hoping being casual is the right move here, I approach them and throw open the door.

"What's up, boss? Security drama this early?"

Both Brix's and Harley's eyes widen at my presence.

"No," Harley says at the same time Brix says, "Yes."

Harley backhands his partner in the stomach. Brix doesn't even pretend to flinch from it.

"No drama at all," Harley says. "Jamie was supposed to meet us in our room half an hour ago. She's never late."

"I can explain," Jamie says. "It's ... not what it looks like ..." She turns to me, smiles, and then glances back at them. "Actually, it's exactly what it looks like, but it's none of your business. Sorry I was late."

I hope she didn't feel like she had to say that for me. Or out herself. I was going to cover for her. Say I stayed here the night for ... well, any number of reasons women who are friends stay at each other's places.

Harley puts his hands up. "No problem here. We were just worried about you. But this, yeah, this makes sense."

Brix glares at me. "It would make sense ... if it were any other member of Mike Bravo. This is ... this doesn't make sense at all."

I want to protest that because it's shitty to hold the men on my team to a different standard than me, but I don't really have a leg to stand on there. We did have sex.

Brix can have his hissy fit, I don't care.

"We're going to need a moment," Brix says, and

I don't know if he means him and Harley or him and me.

"Jamie, I really need you." Harley grabs Jamie's wrist. "Assist me, *assistant*." He stalks away, dragging her with him. She got up at some point and got dressed in a pair of sweats and a tank top. It's so casual to how she has been dressing while on tour, and it reminds me of that night she sat across from me in a bar.

Just before she disappears with Harley, she gives me a quick glance over her shoulder.

I try to force a smile, but my face muscles don't cooperate. Hers do, though, and I let out a small breath of relief at her gorgeous smile.

"Explain yourself," Brix says.

I lift one shoulder. "Late night working. Too tired to go to my own room. Girls' slumber party."

Brix's dark gaze narrows. "You slept with your mark? Wait, I don't think I want to know." He follows after where Harley and Jamie disappeared to while grumbling something about finally knowing how Trav feels.

"Love the pep talk, boss!" I call after him.

---

*Maggie:*
  *SOS.*
  *Me:*
  *Where are you?*
  *Maggie:*
  *The sad excuse for a playroom this venue has set up for the kids.*
  *Me:*
  *Be there in ten.*

Maggie is an amazing woman, and when I met her a couple of years ago at a party for Brix that Harley threw, we instantly clicked. Probably because we're both ex-military. She's someone whose career was admirable. She didn't choose between being a mom and having a career. She had Kaylee and still served, and while she's out of the military now, she left on her terms. Not everyone gets that.

I find her where she said she'd be, but while baby Riff is mesmerized by the lights and sounds coming from the hanging mobile on his playmat and Kaylee is on her iPad, Maggie is pacing back and forth in only a bra and a long hippie skirt.

"What's the emergency?" I ask.

"I have nothing to wear."

"So you messaged your lesbian friend whose closet consists of leather and not much else?"

"I'm desperate."

"Why? Don't you usually just hang backstage out of view?"

"Ryder and Lyric have been telling me to take something for myself, and they've gotten into my head. So, I'm going to do it. With Andre—uh, Domino."

Shit. I mean, yay for them, but also shit. Because I am not good at this. Fashion and dating a man and anything that has to do with any of that.

I haven't seen Jamie since she left her room this morning, but I've seen her wardrobe. She would be better at this than me. Though her clothes won't fit Maggie. Jamie is impossibly petite. Mine will, but I can't even dress myself for a date, let alone someone else. So I take out my phone and text Jamie.

*Me:*

*Are you at the venue or still at the hotel?*
Jamie:
*Hotel but about to head over. Where's my bodyguard?*
;)
Me:
*Already at the venue. Bad bodyguard.*

I hesitate before typing out this next part but decide to say fuck it. I can't spend the next five or so weeks walking on eggshells.

*I'll make sure I guard all of your body later, but I need a favor. Can you break into my hotel room and bring some date options from my closet? Uh, not for me. For Maggie.*

Jamie:
*Is she finally going to go for it with Domino? Eeee. This is so exciting.*
Me:
*Is it?*
Jamie:
*Yes! She deserves happiness and Domino is a fine specimen of a man.*

Does that make me jealous? I think about it, like truly think about it, and I don't think it does. Domino *is* attractive, and just because Jamie and I slept together, that doesn't mean she can no longer find anyone else hot.

Jamie:
*I mean, I prefer my own bodyguard, but he's all right.*
Me:
*Aww, you're sweet to add that, but it's unnecessary. Appreciated, but unnecessary.*
Jamie:
*I'll find Maggie something and see you soon.*

I might not know where we stand after last night, but the flirty texts help. She probably doesn't want anything serious, and, well, neither do I because no one has ever understood my job, but as long as she's not freaking out about her first time with a woman, we're all good here. Even if she decides she doesn't want to do it again and only remain friends. Or friendly. It's not like we're actual friends … are we?

There aren't a lot of female influences in my life. My mom passed when I was young, so I was raised by my military father. The only times I had that motherly figure were the times my abuela would visit or I'd be sent to stay with her in the Dominican Republic for my summer breaks.

I'm not saying my lack of feminine energy is the reason I have more guy friends than women, but it's a theory.

I'd consider Maggie my friend, but we've never actually hung out outside of the band or Mike Bravo. I haven't offered her a couch to sleep on like I did Jamie, so does that mean Jamie is basically my bestie now?

"Jamie's on her way," I say to Maggie. "She's going to pick something from my wardrobe and bring it over."

"I'm not sure dressing like a dominatrix lesbian is the right image for me."

I burst out laughing. "Not a dominatrix, and I can't decide if you're complimenting me or insulting me."

"Definitely complimentary. You're probably the prettiest badass I know, and I envy you. But I don't think I can pull off that look. I'm a frumpy mother who is covered in baby spit-up the majority of the time. I still don't fit into my pre-Riff clothes, and I just … don't feel sexy."

Yet another reason bearing children is not for

me. The hormones, the body changes, and the insecurity about all of it don't sound fun.

"I know telling you that you're gorgeous the way you are probably won't do anything because you're in your head, but you have to remember you gave birth only five months ago. Don't buy into the toxic notion that was probably made up by a man that you need to go right back to how your body was before you had Riff."

She purses her lips and nods. "You're right."

"I know I am."

"Oh, I meant about whatever you're saying not making me feel better."

I sigh.

Her phone pings, but when she reaches into her bag on the floor and reads the message, she mutters, "No, no, no." Her shoulders visibly deflate. "Our nanny has a fever. She thinks she caught what Riff had last week."

"I've heard children are like Petri dishes." I'm not being helpful, I know.

"Okay, this is the third sign I shouldn't throw myself at Domino."

"What were the other two?"

"Nothing to wear, and I don't want to."

I try not to laugh at her because she seems to really be struggling with this, but it's kind of cute the way she's throwing a tantrum over it. I would offer to watch the children for her—I may not want kids of my own, but it's not like I hate them or anything—but with Jamie working the show tonight, I can't leave her side.

Riff starts fussing from where he is, and Maggie mindlessly picks him up, walks over to the couch, and flops out her boob so he can eat.

"I'm going to be alone forever," she says.

I sit on the couch opposite her. "We could be alone together."

Now it looks like it's her turn to cover a laugh. "From what I hear, you weren't alone last night." She smirks.

Of course everyone already knows. "It was nothing."

"Does Jamie know that?"

"I don't know what Jamie knows. We didn't get a chance to talk about it, and I haven't seen her since she left with Harley this morning."

"Damn. We should start a lonely losers club."

"Wow, way to make us sound sad and pathetic."

Normally, I wouldn't care if someone called me that, because I'm happy being single, where there's no drama. But after last night, after Jamie, I think maybe something more with her wouldn't be so bad. A second date, at least.

# CHAPTER EIGHT_

JAMIE

Usually when I'm in crisis mode, it's because Harley is having a diva meltdown and is demanding M&Ms while also asking me to ration them for him. I have to say, this kind of crisis is a breeze.

"It's no problem," I say, reassuring Maggie that Angel and I can watch the kids while she goes out with Domino.

"Harley needs you," Maggie says, and I get the impression she isn't worried about leaving her children; she's merely using them as an excuse to hold herself back from something she wants.

"No, he really doesn't. Brix can give him his backstage snacks for once."

"You do so much more for him than that."

"I do, but not while the concert is going. Besides, he's already told me I can have the night off to do it."

"What? When?"

"When I texted him while you've been talking to me."

Maggie cocks her head. "You haven't even looked at your phone."

"Don't need to."

How she has missed my thumbs flying across my screen while we've been talking, I'll never know, but I'll chalk it up to her freak-out over seducing Domino.

Maggie bites her lip.

Angel is in the corner of the room, laying out different combinations of her clothes for Maggie to pick from. I grabbed a few different options for her and tried to pick the most flowy and flattering, but the majority of Angel's clothes are made out of tight material.

I'm not complaining about that. At all. But for Mags, she needs to feel confident because the disheveled mom before me is anything but that right now.

I can't imagine being in her position. She's been single since before Kaylee was born. I've been single for, like, a minute, and I already have an interest in someone else. Having no one for years? It would be so daunting getting back out there.

"Angel and I have got this. I promise."

"Do either of you have experience looking after children?"

"I'm Dominican," Angel cuts in. "I have many cousins I've looked after. Cousins who have their own babies. Kaylee has her iPad, and Riff at this age is basically a lump. He's not crawling yet, is he?"

"No. He's trying but not getting anywhere."

Angel nods. "So, a lump and a zombie preteen with technology. It will be a breeze, and you won't have to worry about a thing."

"And if someone does break in here to kidnap them for ransom, Angel can take them out." I'm joking, though it's one of those jokes that's actually true.

It goes over Maggie's head, and her eyes widen.

I gently grasp her forearm. "I'm joking. No one is coming for your children. Could you imagine if Ryder Kennedy's kids went missing? The Eleven fandom would be able to find whoever took them faster than the FBI."

For the first time since I arrived, Maggie's shoulders relax, and she lets out a chuckle.

"You're right. I have nothing to worry about. Other than Domino laughing in my face and rejecting me."

Angel scoffs. "Never going to happen."

"Agreed." I nod. "From what I hear, he's been inappropriately checking you out ever since he was assigned to you. He's about a second away from falling in love with you."

And the tension is back, but it's not only in her shoulders this time.

"Or fucking your brains out, I mean. Not love. No love." My gaze ping-pongs around the room awkwardly. Kaylee's headphones are on nice and tight, evidently, so at least she wouldn't have heard any of our conversation about her mother getting laid, but still. Oops.

Angel's deep brown eyes meet mine. "You might want to quit while you're ahead." She picks up an outfit and brings it over to Maggie. "Here. Try these on. And just remember that you're going out to have fun tonight and nothing else. There's no pressure. You'll force Domino to dance, claiming he needs to stay close because he's your bodyguard. You'll flirt. You'll forget you have kids for an hour or two. Maybe there'll be a connection, and maybe there won't be, but the important thing is you go out and get to be yourself for a night without all the other bullshit."

Maggie takes a deep breath and then releases it. "You're right. Fuck it. I'm going for it."

As Maggie walks off to the bathroom to change, Angel steps closer to me. "How are you any good at your job? I thought ninety percent of it was calming Harley down."

"It is, but it's easy with him. I go to the most over-the-top possible outcome, exaggerate it, and then he realizes how ridiculous he sounds. How was I to know you shouldn't joke about kidnapping kids in front of their mother?"

Angel shakes her head. "You're lucky you're cute."

I can't help smiling, even though she's trying to insult me.

I've been so busy today, I haven't really had a chance to overthink last night, but standing here with her, all I can picture is everything we got up to. Her sexy body, her powerful thighs as she straddled me.

My cheeks heat at the thought. Butterflies fill my stomach.

We stare at each other, no words passing our lips. My gaze flickers to her lips, and I beg for her to say the first words about last night, but maybe she's waiting for me.

Other than I enjoyed it and want it to happen again, I don't really have anything else to say.

It doesn't occur to me that maybe she might need reassurance until she says, "A-are we cool?"

"I am if you are," I say.

"You're not freaking out?"

"Nope. Are *you*?"

She glances away. "I don't have a reason to."

I never imagined she would be the one to be insecure in our situation, but it's obvious she is, and even though I have no idea how to deal with that, I'm hoping humor will help. "Not even if I say I want you to quit your job and bear my babies while I focus on my career?"

Now it's her turn to go rigid and squirrelly. I am totally missing the mark on my sarcasm today.

"That was a joke," I say slowly.

She's still stiff, her body standoffish. Her eyes narrow as if she's questioning if I'm telling the truth or trying to backtrack.

Maybe Angel is right; I should quit while I'm ahead.

I put my hand on top of her shoulders. "Angel, breathe. Remember when we met in that bar and you'd had that terrible date who said her career was too important? I thought it would lighten the mood. I promise it was a joke."

She nods, but I get the impression she still doesn't believe me.

"If it reassures you any, I recently decided that I don't want kids."

Finally, she relaxes just enough not to be confused with a mannequin. "You don't?"

"It wasn't until I broke up with Raffy that I gave it proper thought. I always assumed that I would have children because it's what everyone does. Like it's a human's default setting. But with my job and with my ambition to become a tour coordinator or even a talent manager, I'd never be home. Why would I put a child through that? And raising them in Hollywood? No, thanks. It's as toxic as it is addictive. And the more I thought about it, the more I realized Harley is basically a child, so I already have a big baby to care for, but as a bonus, he's toilet trained."

Angel takes me by surprise and wraps her arm around me, pulling me against her body hard and fast. I let out a small "Eeep" as she holds me close, which only makes her gorgeous face break out into a wide smile.

"Eep?" she repeats.

"You took me off guard. I wasn't sure if … well, you know … after last night if—"

"If I'd want to do this again?" Angel lowers her lips to my cheek, laying the softest kiss to my skin.

It's like an electric shock down my spine. My core warms, and I nod.

"I want more of last night," she whispers.

I didn't realize how much I needed to hear that until she says it. Because it's exactly what I want. I rest my cheek against hers. "Me too."

# CHAPTER NINE_

ANGEL

IT'S ENTIRELY POSSIBLE THAT JAMIE Harris is the perfect woman for me. If she really means what she says, anyway. It would be easy for her, someone still in her twenties, to think she doesn't want children now, but from what past flings and dates have told me, something changes once a woman hits thirty. My body must have missed the memo because that biological clock never started ticking for me.

That aside, though, she's supposedly looking for the same kind of situation I am. She wants to focus on her career. I want to focus on mine. But if we could be supportive and active partners when we do have the time, she'd be exactly what I want in a wife.

Though finding enough quality time around our individual work schedules could be an issue for us. Jamie's always doing Harley and band stuff, and I'm being sent all over the world at a moment's notice. But I'm getting ahead of myself anyway. Just because we maybe want the same thing, that doesn't mean we're soulmates or whatever. It doesn't mean she's "the one" I've been wanting to find.

And as I watch Jamie with Maggie's children, how chill she is with them—cooing at Riff while talking to Kaylee about whatever game she's playing on her tablet—I could see her as a mother in the future. I don't want to take that option away from her should she change her mind.

If we were to continue this, get involved, fall in love, and then she decided she did want kids after all, I wouldn't stop her from getting the life she desires. So, I guess the biggest risk I'd be taking by going beyond sex with her is that I might get my heart broken.

Considering I've never found anyone who even had the potential to do that until now, I have to go for it, right?

Jamie picks Riff up off his play mat, but unlike twenty minutes ago when she held him against her and cradled him softly, she's holding him like he's a grenade and she can't get rid of him fast enough. As they get closer to me, I can smell why.

"I don't do diapers," she says in a matter-of-fact way.

I laugh and take the baby off her and head toward the portable change table set up in the room.

Maybe Jamie really won't want kids after all.

Even though I know I'm getting ahead of myself and it's not a good idea to have thoughts of a future with a woman I've spent one night with, I can't help imagining what our relationship could develop into.

It's easy to ignore the logistics and fantasize, and it's even easier to get carried away while dealing with the grossness that is babies. Any distraction from the debris I'm cleaning up from the bomb in Riff's diaper helps.

"Eww, how can you be smiling while you do that?" Jamie holds her nose.

It makes me like her more somehow.

"Years of helping with my younger cousins. Plus, I'm in my happy place up here." I go to tap the side of my head, think better of it because of the diaper and unwashed hand situation, and then drop my hand again.

"Ooh, where's that?"

Of course she had to ask.

"Maybe I'll tell you … one day." I finish up with Riff and put him back down on the floor.

While I turn my back to wash my hands in the nearby sink, Jamie screeches.

I'm not a jumpy person by nature—I can't be in my line of work because one flinch could be the difference between hitting my target and killing the wrong person—but the sound she makes is almost inhuman.

"What? What is it?" I spin to see Riff crawling toward her.

"Maggie said he hasn't done that, right?" She jumps up and down, clapping, her smile lighting up her entire face. Jamie falls to her knees and holds out her arms, and I almost want to get down on the ground and crawl to her as well.

Yeah, I have it bad. And that scares the shit out of me.

Riff reaches her, and she scoops him up and stands.

"Does this mean I'm, like, his favorite human ever? Can I gloat to Ryder and Lyric?"

"I wouldn't if I were you. Actually, let's not mention at all that he decided to start crawling on our watch. Parents live for these first moments ... for some reason."

"Oh. Right. I guess it would have sucked for them to miss it." She cuddles Riff close. "It's okay, cutie. It'll be our little secret."

That doubt I had before comes back because she does look good holding that baby. "Are you sure you don't want kids? You're a natural."

She shakes her head. "God no. Kids are the worst, but the cuddles are pretty good."

"You think I'm the worst?" Kaylee's small voice comes from across the room.

I hang my head. Fuck.

Jamie doesn't miss a beat, turning toward Kaylee. "Oh no, sweetie. Not you. You're awesome. But babies are smelly, and all they do is eat, spit up, and then stink up their stinky diapers. I should've said babies are the worst."

Kaylee smiles. "That checks out."

I laugh because some of the stuff she comes out with sounds so much older than she is.

She goes back to her screen, and I mouth toward Jamie, "Nice save."

Jamie steps closer to me and cocks her head. "Did I pass your test?"

"Test?"

"Yeah. On the whole babies question."

"It wasn't a test. It was ..."

"Seeing if I check all your boxes?" She points at me just as my mouth opens. "And do not make a joke about your box in front of the children." She covers Riff's ears.

I hate that she's calling me out and being so

cute while she does it. It takes all my effort not to fold my arms and pout. I'm not a pouter. But I do owe her some kind of explanation.

"I'm going to level with you."

She steps closer again, resting Riff on her hip. "Mmhmm?" Her eyes are playful, her lips fighting to turn up by the look of it.

"I ..." Why is it so hard to say the words? "I like you, and last night was fun, and I'm trying not to get ahead of myself, but I want ..." *Say it. Just say it already.*

"What do you want?" she whispers.

"I want more. With you. Not only the physical part, but ... more. Even though it's too soon and it's only been, what, a month since you broke up with your boyf—"

Jamie cuts me off with her lips on mine. It's brief, but when she pulls back, she makes my insides dance with anticipation and nerves of the best kind. "Screw too soon. I'm all in. It might not work out. Or it could be the best thing that's ever happened to either of us. You might think I'm not in the right place for something, or I'm still figuring myself out, but leave that up to me. I want to try." She smiles as she recycles my words. "With you."

# CHAPTER TEN_

JAMIE

While waking up next to Angel every day for six weeks, I've been waiting for the novelty of it to wear off. It hasn't. I'm not sure it will.

Some days, like today—the very last day of the Eleven tour—I stare at her, at her soft lips, her golden skin, and the annoying voice that's been invading my brain lately appears once again: she's way out of my league.

This doubt only recently started, and I've been trying to ignore the intrusive thoughts, but they're only getting louder and louder the closer we come to the end of her contract with Eleven.

I'm used to being insecure in relationships—okay, my last relationship—but that had more to do with the way I was treated. Raffy made me doubt myself. Angel has done nothing but treat me like an equal, with respect, and she lets me do my job while she concentrates on her own. I didn't realize I had the idea of a perfect person for me, but I do, and she's it. I think that's why I'm suddenly insecure.

I'm in serious trouble of getting in too deep, which means I could be heartbroken, or worse, I could end up hating her like I hate my ex.

Angel's just so freaking beautiful, and it's impossible to fathom someone who looks like her, is as fearless as she is, and is the most amazing woman I've ever met could be interested in me. And that's not even a low self-esteem thing. I might have insecurities like most people, but deep down, I know I'm fucking awesome. Angel's just awesome-er.

"You're doing it again, weirdo." Angel's dark brown eyes flutter open.

I swear her sniper background gives her a sixth sense when it comes to being watched.

"I can't help it. I'm creepy, what can I say?" Creepy is better than explaining that I think she's too good for me, right? It's better than saying, *I'm in way over my head with you, and I want to hold you close and never let you go after only knowing you for six weeks.*

"Don't you have boy band members to wrangle? Last show and all that." Angel buries her head under her pillow to block out the daylight, but all she's done is remind me that after tonight, we won't have this forced proximity to each other. No obligation. Not that she's had to spend every night with me, but maybe she's been doing it to keep the peace. No messy breakup.

What's to stop her from walking away and saying thanks for the fling? When we started fooling around, she said she wants more, but ... what if she's changed her mind?

And why am I so fucking torn up over it?

When I don't answer her question about wrangling a boy band, she lifts the pillow off her face. "What are you thinking about?"

She must be able to sense it—my doubt. Or know that I'm too in my head to answer her simple question about work.

Abort, abort! Deflect, deflect! "I'm wondering if we have time to get off before I have to do said wrangling of boy banders."

"Mmm" is all she says, but I feel the heat of her stare on me. That assessing gaze. "That sounds like a lie, but if you want to try to distract me with sex, I'm not going to say no. I won't forget about it, though, so you'll have to tell me eventually." She rolls to face me.

"Eventually works." Or never.

Maybe I can drag out the sex until I have to leave and then be super busy all day so we don't get a chance to talk. I could totally hold out.

As if reading my mind, Angel gives me an evil smile, and when she shifts so she's on top of me, kissing her way over my neck and moving down, I realize there's no way I could hold out. Not with her. She pulls down the front of my tank top to expose my breasts and teases a nipple with her tongue. Angel has worked out exactly how to drive me crazy and get me going and how to do it in the least amount of time. I'm desperate before she even reaches my stomach, still tasting my skin with her tongue and now using her hand to palm my breast.

*Come on, Jamie. Hold out, hold out, hold out.*

Angel pulls down my sleep shorts and lifts my feet to slide them all the way off. Instead of putting both feet back down, she shifts so one of my legs goes over her shoulder. My breath catches when she lowers her head. The second her mouth closes over my clit, I know it'll be over all too soon, and then I'm going to have to tell her the truth.

I'm falling for her.

Angel's on a mission to break me, and she's going to break me as fast as possible.

Maybe this is the real reason I don't want things to change now that the tour is ending. She's the only person I've ever been with who can get me so close to coming within a minute of feeling her touch. Her mouth on me.

One finger slips inside me, and another follows a few seconds later. She sucks on my clit, sending sparks through my entire body.

She doesn't slow down, she doesn't take it easy, and while our sex life has been more than eye-opening and a fun exploration for me, this is a whole new level.

I let out a string of curses as I contract around her fingers, and she pushes me over the edge. I swallow my moans, my gasps, and try not to let her see how ruined I am because of her.

It doesn't work. "Fuck," I cry out and slump back against my pillow. "You don't play fair."

She kisses her way back up my stomach and rests her chin just above my belly button. "So, what were you thinking about?"

I sigh and run my hand over her cropped hair. "I … I guess I'm overthinking what happens tomorrow."

Angel lifts up completely now. "Tomorrow? You get a fucking day off. Finally."

"Are you forgetting I live with Harley? Unless I find a place to hide out or move into, I'll be at his beck and call."

It's subtle, but I feel it when her whole body goes rigid on top of me. "Is this your way of asking to move in with me?"

Shit. It did sound that way. Or at least hinting at letting me stay with her. "What? No. No, no, no. I just realize how that sounded. Moving in is—"

"Too soon."

I nod. "Agree. Way too soon. But … I mean, I do want us to continue to see each other."

"Is that what you're worried about? That I'll ghost you as soon as you're no longer my duty?"

"Well, not … *worried*, but it might have crossed my mind. If we could maybe have a few days where I'm free of Harley, where I could stay over at yours because I don't have a new apartment yet … but I'm not asking for more than that. I know you're hesitant about getting serious."

"I'm not hesitant! I'm … cautious."

"Is there a difference?"

"Yes. There is. And to prove it, not only can you come stay with me for a few days, I'll even give you a week."

The sigh that leaves me is heavy with relief, though I'm not sure it should be if Angel's only offering this to prove me wrong. Eh, that can be one-week-from-now Jamie's problem. I just bought myself at least seven more days of Angel.

# CHAPTER ELEVEN_
ANGEL

When I'm woken by the jingling of keys, I assume Jamie has gotten a call from Harley at stupid o'clock, and she's either coming or going, but when I'm conscious enough to feel her still beside me, I'm on high alert.

I'm reaching for a weapon strapped under my bed when a figure appears in the doorway.

"Calm down," Proxy says. "It's just me." There's only one reason he'd be here in the middle of the night.

I sit up and whisper, "We got a job?"

"Spontaneous training mission, so no rush, but Trav knew you'd have your phone notifications off."

He's right about that. I wake so easily that I have to turn my phone off to sleep. Trav understands if I don't get a message late at night. If it's a real emergency, this is what happens. They send someone to get me. Any of the others would've just banged on the door until they woke me. Proxy has a key. Which I am now regretting giving to him.

"Make me some coffee while I get dressed." I slowly climb out of bed, and Jamie barely stirs.

Unlike me, she sleeps heavily. Probably because she's exhausted by the time she leaves work each night.

She throws her whole self into her work, and it's not because she loves Harley Valentine unconditionally—although she does. Jamie has ambition and drive, and I fucking love that about her. I love a lot of things about her, and it's hard to believe that it was less than a year ago I was in this very room, trying to find something to wear to go on a terrible date and whining about wanting to find "the one." I didn't actually believe she was out there.

Everyone else gave me a reason to walk away. Jamie ... it's as if the universe was listening and gave me everything I've ever wanted.

Reluctantly, I put on my gear, grab my boots, and head out to the kitchen, where Proxy's already sitting at my dining table, sipping coffee. There's a full cup in front of an empty seat.

"You're the best." If it wasn't so scalding hot, I'd drink it down in one gulp.

"Liar. You've replaced me."

I lift my cup. "With coffee? Honey, there was never a competition. It's always been coffee."

He places his hand on his chest. "Really feeling the love here, but no, I meant with ..." He nods in my bedroom's direction.

"You're my best friend. She's my girlfriend. I love you both in very different ways. Be thankful for you and your ace ass that's the case."

"My ass isn't the only thing that's ace. It's my dick too."

I shudder. "Don't need to know."

"Seriously, though," Proxy says. "You went from zero to sixty with Jamie in two seconds. She's more than your girlfriend."

"What do you mean?"

"You're living together. She should at least have partner status. Life partner? She's lasted five months longer than any of your other … I wouldn't even call them relationships."

"What? We're not living together. She just stays over a lot because she never found an apartment she liked."

Proxy snorts. "A lot? She's been here every single night since the Eleven tour ended. Even when *you* haven't been here."

I purse my lips. "Well, yeah, but only because I usually get someone to water my plants while I'm gone, and this way, two birds and all that."

Proxy cocks an eyebrow at me and waits.

Now that I really think about it and try to pinpoint the last time she spent a night anywhere but my apartment … "Holy shit, we live together."

Proxy nods. "You full-on lesbian'd her."

I frown. "I did not."

"Angel, baby, sweetie, honey. You became your worst nightmare, and you didn't even know it was happening."

"I've become a stereotype. Minus the U-Haul because she never moved her stuff in, but still."

"Mmm." Proxy sips more of his coffee. "I love your new coffee maker, by the way. Tell me, where did you get it again?"

This is a trap. "Okay, it's hers, but she was right when she said it was better than mine, and it was only taking up space at Harley's house in a box. It makes sense that she offered to …"

Proxy starts laughing so hard and loud that I'm sure it'll wake Jamie up, but as I realize the coffee maker isn't the only thing she's brought into the house with that same excuse, it becomes apparent that she really has moved in. She even has a drawer on her side of the bed and a section of my closet, but she doesn't store a lot there. Only the clothes she wears on a daily basis. For events and things where she has to accompany Harley, like gowns and black-tie stuff, they're all still at Harley's house.

So, she has moved in, technically, but the question is, did she know what she was doing and manipulated the situation, or is she as big a dumbass as I am?

"C-can you tell Trav I'm sick?"

"Are you that afraid of being a stereotype that you're making yourself physically ill over it?"

I want to roll my eyes. "No. But I need to talk to her about this, and I don't see it being a short conversation."

"Why does it have to be a conversation at all? You weren't even aware you were living together. Why is it a problem if you are?"

When he puts it that way, it's not. "I dunno. It's like … she blindsided me."

Proxy laughs again, but softer this time. "If it's any consolation, I don't think she's aware either. Last time I was here, she said she had left something at her place. I'm only pointing it out to you because even though you're in a serious relationship, you still call her your girlfriend like you're casually dating. And hey, if that's how you want to label it, I'm not going to tell you otherwise, but … my Angel is in love, and it's cute. Even if you've abandoned me."

"So dramatic." Yet, I stand and wrap my arms around him from behind and lower my head to his shoulder. "I'm sorry I've been neglecting you."

He pats my hand. "You don't need to be. We're cool."

"Good. Now, if you'll excuse me, I have to wake up my *partner* and yell at her for sneakily moving in." I stand upright again.

Proxy sighs. "Why are you determined to screw this up with her? I wouldn't have mentioned it if I knew you were going to react this way."

"I'm not really going to yell at her. I promise."

He looks relieved, but I grin.

"I'm much scarier when I don't raise my voice at all."

"Jesus H. Christ." Proxy stands. "I'm getting out of here before I become an accomplice to a murder."

"Love you, bye."

He leaves, shaking his head all the way, but as soon as the door closes behind him, I drop the tough-girl act. Am I actually mad that Jamie and I live together and I never noticed? No. At least, not if she is as oblivious to it as I am. But if she moved in on purpose and didn't tell me, that's something entirely different.

I approach my—I guess *our* bedroom—with hesitant footsteps. Do I make a big deal out of this, or do I let it go? I want to let it go, but it's hard when I'll be questioning it until I get an answer. On the one hand, I love having her here, and I want her to officially move in, but what if I ask her and she turns around and says, "What are you talking about. We already live together"?

*Come on, Angel, woman up and tell the girl how you feel.*

Ugh. Feel. Emotions. All that stuff I pretend I don't have when I don't want to face them. The thing that usually gets me to talk about them is watching my dumbass teammates have issues with their relationships because of shit communication. I'm not going to do that.

As Jamie's sleeping form comes into view, I almost don't want to wake her, and that's not my avoidance saying that. She looks relaxed, something rare for her in her line of work. Mine too, really.

We both have high-stress jobs, and it usually takes me a long time to come down from a mission, but coming home to her in the last six months has made it a hell of a lot easier to unwind.

I kneel on the floor by her side of the bed, admiring her makeup-free, smooth skin, her pale lips that are usually a signature bright red. Jamie's beautiful inside and out. She's perfect.

It's in this moment, right here, that I am able to let everything go. It doesn't matter if she moved in on purpose or if it just happened. The important thing is she's here now.

I lean in to wake her with a soft kiss on her cheek.

She stirs, her eyes fluttering open before closing again. "Do you have to go?" she rumbles, her voice thick with sleep.

"I thought I did, but I don't. I ... I have something to ask you."

Her eyes fly open at that, and her gaze flicks

over where I'm on the floor … kneeling. "W-what are you doing?"

I join her in her panic. "Fuck, no. No, I'm not proposing." I jump to my feet. "I was waking you up because Proxy was here, and he pointed something out to me, and I want you to know I'm okay with it."

A cute little frown line appears in her brow. "Okay with what?"

"You. Living here."

Her confusion doesn't let up. "You want me to move in with you?"

"No. Well, yes, but I mean, you already live here."

"What are you talking about?"

"Thank you! That was my reaction when he pointed it out, but Jamie, it's true. You live here."

"All of my stuff is still at Harley's place."

I smile and walk to the wardrobe, sliding open the door. "Is it?"

"They're my work clothes, and it's better if they're hung up so they don't get wrinkly."

Hey, at least we're as oblivious as each other.

Slowly, just as it did with me, it sinks in, and she shoots into a seated position. "Shit. I live here."

That pulls a laugh from me. "Yeah. You do."

"I didn't mean to move in."

Sitting on the side of the bed next to her, I cup her cheek. "I know. Well, I know now. I wasn't sure if you just secretly moved all your stuff in here and hoped I wouldn't notice. Spoiler alert: I didn't even notice, and considering part of my job is attention to detail, you think I would have."

"I can move out if you're freaking out. I can—"

I lean in and kiss her again, this time, dipping my tongue inside her mouth. It's slow and sensual, but it's not about leading to sex. It's about showing her how much I love her.

When I pull back, I whisper, "I want you to live here. Officially."

"You … do?"

"I love you, and it might have happened accidentally, but you belong here. With me."

"I love you too. And I want to be here. With you."

## THANK YOU_

Thank you for reading Angel! While Angel was my first ever FF, I have so many ideas for more. Can't wait to see where my characters take me next.

To read Domino and Maggie's story, flip the book over and start from the beginning.

# ABOUT THE AUTHOR_

Eden Finley is an Amazon bestselling author who writes steamy contemporary romance.
As a socially awkward mess, she likes to lose herself in the written word, reading and writing for pure escapism. Her books aren't supposed to be taken too seriously, and while they sometimes touch on heavy subjects, she will always have a HEA. Because the world needs more of them.

You can follow Eden on any of the following platforms:
https://www.instagram.com/finley.eden/
https://www.facebook.com/EdenFinleyAuthor/
https://www.facebook.com/groups/absolutelyeden/
https://amzn.to/2zUlM16
https://www.edenfinley.com

# THANK YOU_

Thank you for reading Domino!

I always love revisiting the Famous series, and adding the chaos that is Mike Bravo to the mix makes it a lot of fun.

To read Angel and Jamie's story "Angel", flip the book over and start from the beginning.

9 781922 743602

# DOMINO

A MIKE BRAVO OPS SHORT

EDEN FINLEY

# CHAPTER ONE_

DOMINO

"Daddy Andre!"

I hear Riff's screams from down the hall while I do the dishes. A minute later, my wife appears from the direction of his bedroom.

"He wants you."

"Oh no!" I cry. "Then I won't get to finish these dishes."

Maggie shakes her head at me. "I don't know what you bribed him with, but it worked, so you better go pay up, *Daddy Andre.*"

My family refuse to call me by my call sign, Domino. With the other women I've been with, it felt … off to be called by my given name. Too personal. But with Maggie, it's different. It always has been.

Maggie is everything I never knew I was missing in my life. Her exasperated smile makes me weak in the knees. Her loving nature makes me protective of her.

I kiss her on the cheek as I pass her, and her green eyes shine up at me in amusement. Her silky

brown hair smells like vanilla, and the sooner I get the kidlet to sleep, the sooner I can take her to bed.

I lean against the doorjamb of Riff's bedroom and fold my arms. "What are we prolonging bedtime with this time?"

He giggles. Riff was only a baby when Maggie and I got together, so he's grown up with me as a father figure. One of three father figures he has in his life. He calls me Daddy Andre, while his older sister Kaylee only calls me Andre.

I see Kaylee as more than a stepdaughter, but I respect her decision to leave the dad monikers up to her biological dad and his husband.

"I want you to tell me a story," Riff says. He's so cute with his floppy light brown hair and bright blue eyes.

"Mommy couldn't tell you a story?"

"I like your stories. Yours have explosions and killing bad guys."

I put my finger to my lips. "Shhh. Mommy might hear you."

To say that when Maggie and I first got together I knew nothing about kids is an understatement, and even though everyone told me I'd get used to it —that some paternal gene would kick in—I'm still waiting for it to happen five years later.

And telling Riff about my days as a motherfucking badass and army ranger is at the top of the list of why my stories are not the most appropriate for children.

"But they're only stories. They're not true," Riff says.

At least he thinks they're all fiction.

I approach his bed and pull up his blankets be-

fore sitting beside him. "What tale did you want to hear tonight?"

"Umm ..."

"Ooh, what about the time I saved Mommy from a swarm of boyband fanatics?"

His lips purse. "Mommy says she's the one who saved you."

"I mean, I don't want to tell a six-year-old that his mommy lies, but she does."

He laughs. "I think *you're* lying."

I mock gasp and hold me chest. "Me? Never."

"Okay then. Tell me the story."

"To do that, I should probably go back to the very beginning. To the night we met."

Riff shifts and wriggles down to get comfy. "I'm ready."

"I'm sorry," Maggie says from the doorway, making us both jump. "Did I hear you say you were going to tell our son the story of how we met?"

"And how he saved you from Daddy's fans."

She folds her arms. "Oh, hell no. If there's going to be a story. It's going to be told right." She joins us, sitting on the other side of Riff than me.

I smile over at her. "All right then. You want to go first or shall I?"

"Me obviously."

"Then by all means ..."

# CHAPTER TWO_
MAGGIE

THE WHOLE CO-PARENTING THING WAS harder the second time around. With Kaylee, everything was simple. I was serving in the army, so Ryder had full custody. It wasn't ideal, and I missed her like crazy, but serving was something I had to do. Being in the army gave me a purpose, got me out of the small-minded Texas town I grew up in, and I loved it. It gave me opportunities I'd only ever dreamed of—traveling the world, getting a college degree on Uncle Sam's dime—but the biggest impact it had on me was giving my first taste of what love felt like. True love.

And then it was ripped away from me.

Months after John's passing, I was back in that Texan small town, hating life, hating the world, and wanting blood and payback for the IED that took John from me.

Enter Ryder Kennedy, a boy I grew up with. The one who went out and got himself famous by singing in a boy band. In a moment of weakness,

we came together as old friends seeking comfort in each other.

He was the one who brought me Kaylee.

We parented well together, mainly because I was back on tour overseas with the army, and he had nannies to look after our daughter. He took a shining to one nanny in particular. A manny, Lyric. Ryder's interest in men wasn't a huge secret, not even when we made Kaylee—the public didn't know but those closest to him did—and Lyric was an amazing human who I trusted around my daughter.

But going from coparenting with one other person, to deciding to have another child with Ryder through IVF this time instead of the old-fashioned way, I didn't take into account that Riff would be equally Lyric's as he would Ryder's and mine. That was the deal, and I was fully on board. Until it left me outnumbered when it came to big decisions.

They were both great dads, but when they wanted to bring both Kaylee and Riff on a music tour with them, they outvoted me and disagreed it would be disruptive to their routines.

Which is how I ended up, at thirty-one, following a boy band around the country with two kids in tow.

I was a goddamn solider in the US Army reduced to … a groupie. Even though that wasn't the actual situation, it sometimes felt like it. Especially when the band hired a bodyguard for me and the kids' protection.

A *bodyguard.*

For the kids, I understood. For me? It was suffocating.

Ryder entered his living room where I had

adorable little five-month-old Riff in a Baby Bjorn, trying to get him to go to sleep by bouncing him up and down.

"Are you still sulking because I'm forcing you to come on tour or because we hired you a bodyguard for it?"

My scowl deepened. "Both. Plus, your son is being fussy."

"No, no, we've already been over this. When he's happy, he's my child. When he's not, he's either yours or Lyric's. That's how this works." Ryder grinned wide, his blue eyes that matched Riff's shining.

I snorted. "That's right. It's all Lyric's and my fault even if fifty percent of Riff's genes came from you. Totally works."

"Yup." He winked.

"Have I reminded you lately how much I hate you?" I was joking. I loved Ryder to death in a platonic life-partner kind of way.

"Every day," he said in an exasperated tone. "Twice a day since I told you about the tour."

"Good. As long as you don't forget."

Ryder held out his arms. "Okay, give me my son. I'll get him to sleep. You go change your clothes. Maybe put on something that doesn't have baby spit up on it?"

"Why?" I handed over the baby.

"Your new bodyguard is on his way over."

"And I need to look nice for him, why? Didn't you go to that all-queer firm Harley is friends with?"

Ryder grinned again, only this time, there was something evil in it.

"What did you do?" I asked.

"I might have maybe, possibly, asked for the only straight guy on their team to be assigned to you?"

"I really do hate you, Ryder Kennedy," I muttered.

"Come on. It's been forever since you've even been on a date. You deserve a relationship again. You deserve happiness."

I didn't want another relationship. I knew I would never love again. Not after losing John.

I loved Ryder and Lyric like family, because that's what they were. There was nothing between Ryder and me, and he and Lyric we perfect for each other. But even when Ryder and I were together that one fateful night, what we shared wasn't the kind of passion and love that I had with John. It was, at most, companionship.

What I had with John was a rare kind of love that I knew would never come again.

So it was tiring when Ryder or Lyric tried to set me up with someone.

"If this bodyguard can't see past a little spit-up, I guess he's not the man for me. What a shame. Oh no."

Riff, the damn traitor, was already asleep in his father's arms.

"We just want you to be happy," Ryder whispered.

"I am happy. I'm a strong, independent woman who don't need no man."

"You might not need someone, but it's nice to not be alone. Before Lyric ..." He shook his head. "I don't know how I did the whole celibacy and alone thing."

"I have Bob, and he's all I need."

Ryder frowned. "Who's Bob?"

"My battery-operated boyfriend. B-O-B."

Ryder's gaze flicked above my head, and then Lyric's voice came from behind us.

"And we just came in at the wrong time. Or, at least, I hope it was the wrong time because I don't want to know."

I rolled my eyes and turned to Lyric, but my reply died on my lips when I saw the man standing next to Lyric.

Dark hair, gorgeous brown skin and warm eyes. Muscular. A soldier's physique. A soldier's cocky smirk on his lips too. My heart skipped a beat, and warmth shot through me.

Familiarity.

That's when it hit me. I knew this man.

"Mags, this is Domino," Lyric said.

I shook my head. That wasn't his name. It was … it was … It was on the tip of my tongue.

He stepped forward, his imposing stature making my body react in a way it hadn't done in years. I almost got my hopes up that Ryder and Lyric had done good this time, but I should've known it wouldn't last.

Because as Domino reached his hand out for me to shake, and we made that connection, I remembered where I knew him from.

"Andre. Staff sergeant Andre Martinez," I whispered.

He cocked his head. "Have we met?"

"Ooh, please tell me he was your superior officer back in the day," Ryder asked, way too excitedly.

And no, he wasn't.

"You served?" Sergeant Martinez asked. "I would've remembered if you were under me."

Lyric snickered.

"I mean under my command." Martinez's eyes were comically wide, and I somehow found it charming.

But then reality bit at me again, and I shook my head. "You weren't my commanding officer."

He was John's.

# CHAPTER THREE_
DOMINO

The woman standing before me was a vision. Even with the baby puke all over her shirt, her hair a mess, and the conflicting emotion across her face.

It wasn't until she told me who she was that it clicked I'd seen her before.

"You were John Libsy's CO, and I was—"

Oh shit. "His Maggie." I'd seen countless photos, heard endless stories, and practically knew her already because of it.

She nodded solemnly.

Even though it had been over ten years since John was under my command, and he'd lost his life not long after being transferred out of my unit, I hadn't been able to go to his funeral. I was on doing my third tour of Afghanistan.

"I'm sorry for your loss."

She forced a smile that didn't reach her eyes. "It was a long time ago. My life took a bit of a detour after he passed."

I glanced around the large mansion, the famous

person Maggie shared children with, and noticed the vast difference between her life now and what it would've been like back when she was with John. "I'd say detour might be an understatement."

Her face lit up, and I immediately knew I was screwed.

My gaze ping-ponged between Ryder Kennedy and Lyric Jones. I knew they were together, and Maggie was their child's mother, but where Maggie fit in with them in a relationship sense was less obvious.

"Well, then," Ryder said. "This little guy needs to be put in his crib." He lifted the baby up to kiss the top of his head. "Lyric, come help me."

"Help you?" Lyric's nose scrunched. "What, you worried you're going to throw him in there or something? Suddenly forget how not to drop a baby?"

They bickered back and forth as they made their way down the hall, leaving Maggie and me alone.

The tension was thick between us, but I couldn't read the vibe. Was I attracted to her? The immediate gut reaction to her said yes. I could've sworn I saw a flicker of interest on her side too. Until she realized who I was.

John wasn't under my command when he was blown up by that IED, but I didn't think that would matter to Maggie.

I could remember all the stories John told us about her. How he said he was going to marry her one day. They were going to be together forever, and that she was *the one*.

"This is … weird," she said, tucking a rogue piece of hair behind her ear.

"If you want a new bodyguard, I'd total under-

stand. There are five of us assigned to the tour, and—"

"I never wanted a bodyguard to begin with, but if I have to have one, you'd be the best pick."

I cocked my head. "Without sounding like I'm fishing here, why would I be the best pick?"

Her eyes turned sad. "Because John trusted you with his life. It means you don't have to earn my trust. You already have it."

Well, damn.

In this business, carrying out a protection job was always referred to as babysitting. I had been tailing Maggie and her kids for a week already—ever since the lead up to the tour began getting fan-crazy—and at every turn, she took babysitting to a whole new level just to frustrate me.

Tonight was the first show of the tour, and she was still being stubborn.

"Please let me carry something?" I asked Maggie who had the baby strapped to her chest while carrying a diaper bag on one shoulder, pushing a stroller, and holding Kaylee's hand with her singular free hand.

"But how will you stop all the bullets if you're wearing a diaper bag? What will that do for your masculinity?" She gasped.

Maggie was snarky. A smoking hot, snarky, competent, smartass.

"Bullets?" Kaylee looked up at her mother. Though, she wouldn't be looking up for long. She was only eight but was already up to Maggie's shoulder.

Maggie smiled and patted her daughter's head. "I was just being silly. No one would shoot at us."

It was true. Mostly. Other than a close call with a stalker, Harley Valentine hadn't ever seen violence from a fan, and he was the most famous one out of the boy band.

Though, all of them were household names when it came to Eleven. Their solo careers were a different story.

"Then why do we need him?" Kaylee nodded toward me.

Hey, kid, if it was up to me, I wouldn't be here either, but with Trav away, and half of the team on assignment, there wasn't any other option. Harley's partner Brix used to be one of us, but he left to head up Harley's security team. His guys were all on other jobs because this music tour wasn't exactly planned. It was an impromptu idea they came up with on vacation when talking about their next album. It was supposed to be a year out at least. But when a boy band gets together and drinks, they come up with really stupid ideas. And then post it on socials.

According to Brix, it had been a rough month, throwing together everything for this tour. Sets, security, roadies, venues.

He asked for a favor, and Mike Bravo always had each other's backs, even if they weren't members anymore.

I knelt down to Kaylee's level. "I'm only here to make sure none of those annoying photographers

outside the arenas get pics of you or accidentally step on your toes or hurt you while trying to get images to sell to the tabloids."

"Paparazzi are annoying," she said.

"They sure are," I agreed.

"We ready to go watch your daddy's show?"

Kaylee nodded, and she was so cute I wanted to boop her on the nose, but I refrained. That would've been weird. Just because she reminded me of a young Maggie but with innocence and outrageous eight-year-old things she had said, it still would've been weird for me to act ... fatherly. She already had two of those.

We made our way out to the car, Maggie still refusing to let me help her with all the baby crap.

"You know, the whole strong independent woman thing doesn't mean doing everything yourself and refusing help," I pointed out.

"It's not part of your job," she reminded me.

So instead of helping her, I stood there watching and feeling completely helpless.

How was it possible even her stubbornness was a turn on? I might have felt like a lazy-ass, but it was fun to watch Maggie be so determined.

There were moments. Brief fleeting moments where I could've sworn I caught her staring at me, but I was sure that was wishful thinking on my part.

I couldn't get over how stunning she was. How ... put together she was yet I could see the sadness inside her. The longing for a man who died ten years ago.

The way John used to talk about her, I got the impression she was this lively, strong-willed woman. And while her will wasn't gone, that brightness he would brag about was.

It shone in moments with her kids. When she would get playfully exasperated with Ryder or Lyric. But it was always temporary.

I wanted to make her shine brighter for longer.

Indefinitely.

Turning down being Maggie's bodyguard would have been the smart thing to do—conflict of interest and whatnot—but her putting so much trust in me because of how John saw me all those years ago, I weirdly felt like I owed it to John.

I wasn't sure how he would react if he knew I was checking out his woman, though. Whenever I found myself trailing my gaze over her from head to toe, I'd look up to the sky afterward and send up an apology to him.

Maggie finally got the car all packed, Riff strapped to his car seat, and she climbed into the back of the Escalade with Kaylee. It was one of those modified rides for celebrities where the back seats faced each other instead of the front, and when I glanced back in the rear view mirror, I could see Maggie and Kaylee.

I had to force myself to watch the road and not Maggie or the headlines might have risked reading "Bodyguard kills Ryder Kennedy's family in fatal car crash."

That was not life goals.

I pulled up to the arena, where the Eleven boys were already rehearsing for tonight's show and let Maggie and the kids out by the loading dock where Brix was waiting to take over from me while I parked the car.

By the time I made it inside and found them, Kaylee was onstage with her dad and Riff was asleep in Lyric's arms.

Maggie was nowhere to be found.

I approached Jamie, Harley Valentine's assistant. "Have you seen Maggie?"

"Yeah, she stole Harley's new bodyguard."

I frowned. She wanted to fire me? "Should I be offended?" I try to joke.

"Oh, not like that. I think they're just talking in the band's dressing room. You know ... army chick stuff." Jamie's cheeks flushed, but I didn't read into it.

"I'll let them have their talk then." Though, I wasn't entirely sure what to do with the kids being preoccupied and Maggie being with Angel.

Angel could handle anything that came at them. Fans who snuck in, stalkers ... Hell, knowing Angel, she would've protected Maggie against an innocent stagehand. That poor guy.

Yet, when Angel came into the backstage area alone, I cocked my head at her.

"You're not with Maggie?"

She smiled. "I was. She's alone in there now though. Maybe you should go make sure she's not being attacked by jealous groupies."

"Are there a lot of those in the dressing room?"

"Hundreds. I barely escaped with my life," she deadpanned.

I tried to hide my smile but failed. "Guess I should go do my job then."

"Yes, you should. And do it well." Angel winked.

Okay, I knew I wasn't exactly being subtle when it came to checking out Maggie, but it couldn't have been that see through ... right?

Angel went to stand beside Jamie, and they smiled at each other in a way that let me know they had a secret. Or shared a secret.

Was it about Maggie? Did they know something I didn't?

I headed for the dressing room where Maggie

was supposed to be, but she wasn't in there. The bathroom door was closed, so I went to check in there before searching the rest of the building. Maggie made it well known she didn't want a security detail, and knowing the kind of women I served with in the army, I wouldn't have put it past her stubborn ass to skip out. Her kids were with their dads, plus had me overlooking them, so if she wanted to leave, she could have. Hell, Angel probably helped her. Sisters in arms and whatever.

But when I reached the bathroom and raised my hand to knock, the door flung open, and Maggie spilled outside. She flinched at my presence, but I was too stuck on what she was wearing to do anything about it.

Holy damn. She'd changed into tight leather pants and a glittery black top that tied at her neck and a tiny string behind her back. Her hair was in a military braid, tight and low.

Considering she'd only given birth six months ago, she looked damn phenomenal. She was still carrying some of the baby weight around her stomach, but it was sexy as fuck. *She* was sexy as fuck.

My mouth hung open, but instead of finding my blatant ogling inappropriate like she should've, her lips twitched upward.

"What? Didn't realize I had real clothes that weren't covered in spit up?"

Sure. That was why I couldn't tear my gaze away from her. "Are you going out onstage or something?"

She laughed. "Nope. Just ... felt like looking good. It's been a while."

I frowned. "Lies. You look good every time I see you." I wasn't just saying that either.

From the moment I walked into Ryder Kennedy's house and saw her in dirty sweats, her hair a mess, she was the most beautiful woman I'd ever seen. Did she look good in her dressy clothes? Of course. But I didn't care about the clothes.

Ugh, there I went again. I stared up at the roof and whispered, "Sorry, brother."

"What was that?" Maggie asked.

"Nothing." My voice cracked.

She didn't believe me. I got the impression she knew exactly what she was doing. Especially when she turned and bent over the couch, reaching for her leather jacket on the opposite side.

I had to chant in my head. *"Do not objectify a fellow soldier. Do not objectify a fellow soldier. As my old CO used to say, no hooking up with your battle buddy."*

It didn't work. I had so many thoughts, so many fantasies, running through my mind.

She was smiling at me, but if she knew what I was thinking about, she probably would've slapped me. I wouldn't have blamed her.

I didn't know what it was about Maggie. It wasn't as if we'd had any deep conversation or anything. But it was as if I knew her. Or, I knew John's version of her.

I wanted to see that woman. Bring her out of the shell she had put herself in since John's passing and becoming a family woman.

"It's almost a shame for you to get all dressed up when you won't be seen hanging backstage."

Her smile was back, mischievous this time. I couldn't tell if I was nervous or excited at what she had in mind. I should've been scared. I was responsible for her life, and if anything happened to her, I was sure the Eleven boys would hire a hitman.

Hell, Brix, my old teammate, my subordinate, would probably volunteer for it if Harley told him to.

"What are you planning?" I asked suspiciously.

"Well, like you said. It would be a waste to let all this remain unseen. So, I'm going to the concert."

I thumb behind me. "This concert? In public?"

"Yup. Angel is looking after the kids tonight, and—"

"Wait. Angel Angel? The woman whose name is the Angel of Death? She's looking after your kids?"

"It's okay. Jamie will be with her too, and she's babysat for me before. After Lyric makes an appearance on stage, he'll take over. Plus, Angel says you trust her, and John trusted you, so ..."

"There's that blind trust again." It was daunting. Someone putting that much faith in me when they barely knew me. I appreciated the hell out of it because I knew how hard trust was to earn, but it was a lot of pressure.

I just hoped I wouldn't fuck it all up.

Angel had better protect those kids with her damn life because suddenly, the worst thing that could happen to me was breaking Maggie's trust.

# CHAPTER FOUR_
MAGGIE

I DIDN'T KNOW WHAT THE HELL I WAS DOING listening to Ryder. Or Lyric. Or Jamie. Or … okay, pretty much every member of Eleven, plus their entourage. They were all encouraging me to throw myself at my bodyguard, and I resisted as long as I could.

A week was totally resisting. This man was so … so … I couldn't think of a word for every girl's fantasy of a man. It was an amazing show of self-restraint that I'd made it a whole week without accidentally losing all my clothes.

But maybe they were all right. I needed a night for me, and Domino was the first man since John that piqued my interest.

He had to know I was playing games. That I was trying to seduce him. I could have sworn I saw him checking me out whenever we were together. He was trying to be subtle, but he really wasn't. I thought I even heard him apologize to John once for doing it. That made me laugh.

A genuine laugh.

I laughed with my Kaylee all the time over silly things she thought were funny. I laughed when Riff peed on Ryder and was in stitches when Kaylee asked Ryder and Lyric when they were getting married, and they both had only "Umm" and "Uh" to say in response. But the idea of a man finding me that attractive that he felt he had to apologize for looking?

I hadn't felt that wanted in a really long time.

And it was cute he thought John would care.

Being deployed, we both knew coming home safe wasn't a guarantee. We always said that if something happened to one of us, we were to move on, but when it actually happened, I couldn't see past the devastation of losing him to really notice anyone else.

Domino was the first to turn my head.

And even though it was most likely going to be a fling—what single man wanted to settle down with a mother of two children who she shared custody with a famous person?—I was finally ready to move on.

Dating was horrible, and I hadn't been interested in anyone. Not even enough to even sleep with them. But I was ready to bang the hell out of Domino.

I wanted to feel that connection, that passion I once had.

So, when Domino followed me into the crowd at the overfilled stadium, and we took our spots in a VIP area where it was still crowded but we had enough room to move, I purposefully stood closer to him than probably necessary.

He didn't move away, which could have been

because he was in charge of my safety or because he liked being practically up against me.

Domino's body heat radiated my skin, and slowly, inch by inch, song by song, I closed the miniscule gap and ended up standing in front of him, moving my hips with the songs. My ass brushed over his crotch at least twice before he finally put his hands around my waist to stop me.

"What are you doing?" He whispered in my ear, but it sounded more like a growl.

I didn't pull away and neither did he, so I leaned back, turning my neck to say in his ear. "Dancing. Why do you ask?"

"What's your end game?" he asked.

It made me flinch because none of the men I'd dated or been with had been so blunt. Not even John.

I turned away from the stage and spun to face Domino. The fire in his eyes set my body alight, turning on all those sensitive zones I thought had dried up.

I could have kept playing games with him. I was sure I was supposed to play coy or make him chase me or some other old fashioned bullshit etiquette—but the bottom line was, even if this wasn't going to turn into anything, I could've at least put myself out there for tonight.

I pressed myself against him and leaned into his ear once more. "My end game, to put it bluntly, is to have sex with you."

When I pulled back, his eyes were wide and he was stoic and still.

I kept talking. "When the guys hired you for the tour, they specially assigned you to me in the hopes

we'd hit it off. And I fought them on it every step of the way. Until I met you."

"But John …"

"He died ten years ago. I'm ready to move on. That's not to say I want to move on from him with you or that I'm hoping for flowers and romance and forever or some shit. Right now, all I want is to put almost nine years of celibacy behind me."

Just when I thought his eyes couldn't get wider, they did. "Nine years?" he exclaimed.

I laughed. "I haven't been with anyone since the night Kaylee was conceived."

Domino stuttered. "N-n-nine …"

"If it's too much pressure—"

He blinked out of his trance. "Not too much pressure at all."

This time, it was Domino who closed the small gap between us. He put his hands on my hips, long fingers splayed so close to my ass.

And as he lowered his head, bringing his lips within inches of mine, he said, "I can be that man for you."

I wasn't sure what he meant, but I also didn't care to ask in that moment.

Sex, a night, a week, a tour … I didn't care how long he could give me, just *what* he could give me.

Then it all came crashing down when he said, "But I'm on duty right now."

I wanted to scream in sexual frustration, but instead, I squared my shoulders, looked him dead in the eyes and said, "What did I tell you about not needing a bodyguard?"

We were so close, I could feel the rumble in his chest. The weak protest. The beginning of giving in.

His tongue darted out to wet his sexy mouth, and I bit my bottom lip to stop me from asking to suck on his.

"You're going to get me in trouble." Even though his words were serious, his delivery wasn't. He sounded resigned with a touch of eagerness.

And when he finally relented, he relented hard.

Domino's mouth met mine, firm and strong. It had been so long since I'd even kissed a man. Not as long as since I'd had sex, but still longer than I wanted to admit.

I was a firm believer that a woman didn't need someone to fulfil them. Or complete them. I was raising a daughter, and I wanted her to be independent. While I still believed that with all my heart, Domino could fill me in other ways. Hot, scorching, amazing orgasm ways.

But my life couldn't be that easy. It never was.

On what I'm assuming was a hot mic moment from Lyric getting fitted for his earpiece and mic backstage while he waited to come on, his voice wrung out through the arena.

"Go Mags! Oh, shit."

We pulled apart.

Eleven were onstage, singing one of their hits, but with Lyric's interruption, Ryder broke and laughed, which made Denny snicker. The only one who remained professional was Harley, but even he gave up eventually.

It was only a brief break in the song. A momentary pause where the instrumentals played unaccompanied by voices. Yet, when all five started singing again and the majority of the crowd were back to being fixated on them up on stage, there was that tiny ring of VIPs. The ones who could see

us. Were so close to us, with no barriers cutting us off, that they could scream.

And scream they did.

"Kaylee and Riff's mom!" Someone screamed.

"Who's the guy? Is Riff even Ryder's?" Another voice yelled.

Just what I needed: more shit to swallow from Ryder fanatics. It had been crazy over the years. From being called a fame whore, to getting death threats for being the mother of Ryder's child, it really was an insane industry to be a part of.

Like anything with a fandom attached, ninety percent of the people in it were great. The other ten percent? They lived so far outside of reality that their obsessions were dangerous.

"Still don't need that bodyguard?" Domino asked in my ear.

"Let's get out of here before the claws come out." I took his hand and pulled him toward the barrier where venue security were stationed.

We almost made it there too, but we were cut off.

The next part became hazy, but in my line of sight, it looked like a horde of zombies crowding around us.

Domino wrapped his arms around me, protecting me from the crowd, but we couldn't just stand there all night.

"Okay screw this." Domino scooped me up in his arms and bulldozed his way through the crowd.

I couldn't help laughing because there were a lot better ways to get me out of there, but at the same time, it felt so good to be taken care of in that way.

He carried me as if I weighed nothing all the

way through to the open pathways than lined the arena. Once we got out of the VIP area, he put me down on my own two feet again, but people were still following us. From there, we had to run. Domino held my hand the whole way, refusing to let go.

We dodged people with drinks, people dancing, and made a beeline for the steps to get the hell out of here.

A lot of the rabid fans gave up, but not all of them. We were still being followed, and it was going to be impossible to shake them until we could get back around to the backstage door and show our passes.

It was possible the fans still chasing us just wanted an autograph from me—something I never, ever, ever got used to over the years because I was a nobody—but from my experience, if someone was that desperate to get to me, it was because they didn't think I deserved to have Ryder's babies and had no trouble telling me that to my face.

It got tiresome, and even though all of the Eleven PR crap told me to take it on the chin and ignore that bullshit, sometimes it was hard. But when I spoke out about it, I was whiney and entitled and telling people how they should or should not feel.

It was always a no-win situation, so I didn't want to stick around to find out who was genuine and who wasn't.

Our running must have garnered attention from more people, because once we were on the mezzanine level, it was as if the group chasing us had multiplied again.

Eleven zombie-fans were everywhere.

"I have no idea how to get to the backstage area," Domino said.

I smirked up at him. "Some bodyguard you are."

I, on the other hand, had been to this specific arena many times. I'd chased Kaylee around it when she was younger while the guys rehearsed. Shockingly, an active six-year-old would not sit still and watch a concert, even if it was only a five-minute sound check.

"This way." I led him into dangerous territory, but if we could get passed the bar, it was only a couple of stage doors until there was backstage access.

Only, when we got there, because it was the middle of the concert, the backstage door was un-manned, and we didn't have the swipe cards to get in.

"Shit," I hissed.

"I thought you knew where you were going?" Domino taunted.

Across the way, on the other side, I saw a utility closet. We could have kept running and gone around to the other side of the arena where it was more likely to be someone to let us in, but it was risky.

The more people who saw us, the more chance of being ambushed by them.

The round structure of the building meant we were hidden by those currently chasing us down for now, so before I could change my mind, I pulled Domino toward the closet.

"I do," I said with more confidence than I felt.

It was thankfully unlocked, and when I pushed him through the door, I quickly closed it behind me and flicked the little latch.

Even if anyone did see us coming in here, they would give up eventually.

The concert was still going.

Why chase me when they could see their idols performing the songs they loved?

"This was your plan?" Domino asked while promptly tripping over a mop bucket. The lighting was non-existent.

"It got us away from them, didn't it?"

"Yeah, but now we're stuck inside this room which is smaller than a jail cell for the foreseeable future." He took his phone out, hit the flashlight option, and then propped it up on one of the shelves so we could see.

I stepped closer to him. "I could think of worse people to be stuck with, couldn't you?"

He licked his lips. "Were you always this forward? I swear John said you were this shy, timid thing." He winced immediately, as if thinking the mere mention of John would send me into a spiral, but I lost John years ago now. I'd dealt with it.

By the time I was discharged from the army, I had put John's death behind me, so it didn't hurt to talk about him anymore.

"I was around him," I said. "I was young. But having kids changes you as a person."

"It does?"

I stepped closer again.

He backed up, his large body pressing against the shelves. I should have been offended he was trying to get away from me, having second thoughts about my proposition while we were dancing, but I wasn't.

He was trying to be respectful of John. I knew that.

"When you're a parent, you get so little free time to yourself. Very few chances to get what you want. So you learn to take those moments unapologetically."

We were so close now, that he couldn't move back any farther.

I needed sex so bad. It had been way too long. I wasn't above begging, but I could already see Domino's resolve cracking.

He broke once already, kissing me like he was a starved man and I was the only meal he'd seen in a long time. If I could get him to do it again—

He surged forward and pressed his lips to mine.

It felt so good to have that connection with someone, the sense of needing to be close, to be physical.

Domino's body was something like out of those Magic Mike movies, and it was tempting to rip his shirt off him, but I wouldn't. Him having to walk around shirtless later would draw even more attention to me.

Domino groaned, long and loud, his hips jutting forward. I could feel his hard length push against my abdomen, but I needed it lower. I was too short, and—

As if reading my mind, Domino lifted me so I could wrap my legs around his waist. He spun us so my back was up against the wall, and he was boxing me in.

This was what I wanted. No, this was what I *needed*.

I hadn't felt attraction to anyone like this in recent years. I wanted Domino, and I could feel how much he wanted me.

His cock rubbed against me in just the right spot, sending tingles all over my body.

I wanted more. Wanted him inside me. But I also didn't want to stop this.

It felt too good.

He was still kissing me, his tongue teasing me with its talents that I wouldn't get to experience. At least, not in this dirty closet.

I rubbed my hands all over his wide chest, wanting to feel his tight muscles beneath my fingertips.

Before too long, his lips broke from mine, and he whispered two small, tiny words, that had me melting into him. Falling.

"Want you."

# CHAPTER FIVE_
DOMINO

MAGGIE WAS KILLING ME. HER forwardness was so fucking irresistible, and with her wrapped around me, I was drowning.

Drowning in guilt, drowning in arousal, just ... drowning.

When I whispered how much I wanted her, she shuddered in my arms.

We needed less clothing, fewer barriers.

Maggie lowered her sexy as fuck legs and undid the button on her insanely tight pants. She kicked them off but left her pale pink thong on.

I couldn't do anything but stare down at her, inches of bare skin on display. I was frozen.

That was until she moved on to my pants, gripping the zipper and pulling it slowly down. I undid the button for her, and she took that as an invitation to sink to her knees.

Fucking hell ... this woman.

Her soft hands pulled my cock through the hole in my boxer briefs, and when her sexy, pouty lips

wrapped around the tip, I had to brace my hand against the wall just to control myself.

I was so close to unleashing in her mouth, thrusting to the back of her throat, but I held strong. If this was her only chance to take something for herself, coming way too soon wouldn't have been the ending she was hoping for.

I tapped her shoulder. "If you keep going, it's not going to end well."

She slowly dragged her mouth down my shaft and back up, the wet heat driving me crazy. She gave the tip a little suck as my hips bucked forward on their own accord.

Maggie pulled off and glanced up at me, her big green eyes shining.

She gripped my cock, stroking me. "Do you have ... I mean, do we need ..."

There was the shy girl I'd expected.

"I can't get pregnant, but—"

I always kept a condom on me for times like this—unexpected surprise sex was the best. "I got it." I reached into my back pocket and pulled out my wallet, pulling out the wrapper I had stashed in there, but when I went to open it, she took it from me, opting to do it herself.

She was determined to ruin this for her, like it was a challenge to make me blow before I got a chance to get inside her.

I was determined not to let her win.

It seems both of us were strong-willed.

Even if I had to chant in my head things about Iris's ball sac or the stench of the Mike Bravo basement at HQ where it smells like locker room sweat just to take the edge off a bit.

She rolled the condom down my aching shaft,

and my breathing stilted. She was so tender, so caring.

It made me want to fuck her senseless. Make her unravel.

Once she was done, I didn't give her a chance to tease me some more. I hooked my hands under her arms and lifted her to her feet before picking her up again.

Her legs wrapped around me once more, and I pushed her back against the wall so I could focus on her instead of needing to hold her up.

I wanted to sink inside her so badly, but knew I had to bide my time.

I reached between us, my fingers moving her thong aside so they could find her hole. They played with her opening while my thumb rubbed against her clit.

Maggie threw her head back, exposing her bare throat that made me want to make claiming marks all over it. But that's not what this is. She's made it clear this is her being selfish, and I'm more than willing to give it to her. I can't be selfish in return by painting her neck with hickies, even if I'd love to see her walking around with my mark on her skin.

"Fuck," she hissed and then reached between us, gripping my cock to guide it inside of her.

It was so tight. Warm. It felt ... right. Like two puzzle pieces made to fit together.

My groan was so loud, I swear it echoed around the whole stadium. Exaggerating? Me? Never.

"You feel so fucking good," I breathed against her skin.

"It'll be even better when you start moving." She writhed in my arms, desperate for more.

"Wait up a sec. I don't want this to be over before you get a chance to come."

"Come on, solider."

I pulled back to stare at her, and she smirked at me, her full lips looking so fucking tantalizing.

With a growl, I thrust inside her hard, and her back scraped along the rough wall.

She called out in pleasure or pain, one or the other, but I was determined and focused to prove to her my little soldier could handle her. I couldn't. I was already gone for her. But my cock had to take one for the team and stay focused. At least until I could make her scream and come her brains out.

"More," she moaned.

We had to be fast because I knew it wasn't going to be long before a janitor or other security guards found us. Or worse, fans knocking on the door.

I brought my best work, showing Maggie what she could have if she decided to pursue something more with me in the future.

Sure, there were things in our way. Our connection to John. Her being on tour with a famous band. Me, in a position that would be difficult for her to be okay with ...

I told myself not to think about that and to only think about her. About her pleasure in this moment.

I fucked her against that wall. Fast. Hard. And when she started breathing heavily, her grip flying to hold shoulders and holding tight, I knew she was close.

I was close too. In a last act of desperation to push her over the edge, I reached between us and rubbed my thumb against her clit.

She shuddered and threw her head back, and it was the sexiest thing I'd ever seen. I closed my mouth over her neck, sucking as I pushed myself closer and closer to that edge she was currently falling over.

"Andre" she whispered hoarsely as she came.

I had to pull my hand from between us and slam my palm against the wall to help me keep upright as I erupted inside her.

It was so intense, I had to close my eyes and ride it out.

When I was finally able to settle enough to look at her again, she was leaning back, flush against the wall, and the little smirk on her face was the most beautiful thing I'd ever seen.

I knew in that moment, my life would change.

I saw everything. Every possibility of a future I didn't know I wanted until that very moment.

A wife.

Kids.

A stable job.

Even stability in general.

I saw it all. In her.

# CHAPTER SIX_

MAGGIE

"AND THAT, IS THE STORY OF HOW MOMMY saved Daddy Andre from a horde of screaming fans," I whisper and smile over at Domino.

Domino leans over the twin bed, getting closer to me. "We're so lucky he fell asleep before you went into all the sex in the close detail."

"Mm, that was more for your benefit."

"I should hope so, but now that you've made me harder than fucking steel, what are you going to do about it?"

"I'd love to go take advantage of you in bed, but unfortunately, the story totally cut into doing the dishes. I guess one of us is going to have to go finish them."

My husband's eyes narrow. "By one of us, you mean me, right?"

"And people say men can't read between the lines. Hopefully, you'll finish the dishes before I finish myself off in the shower." I stand and waltz out of the room, laughing as Domino runs down the hall.

I never expected to fall in love with him. Wasn't prepared for it. I wasn't really prepared for anything.

I loved my life, the family I'd built with Ryder and Lyric. The kids were my world, so I never thought … I never thought taking something for myself that one fateful night could lead me to love again.

I wasn't expecting more than sex. For that one night, for a few weeks, I was sure that was all it would be. But it turns out, that night changed everything. It gave me hope. It gave me love again. And after that night, I knew everything would be different for me.

My heart twinges because I'm so grateful for what I have. It almost feels selfish to have two great loves of my life, but without a doubt, Domino is that for me.

He makes my soul complete, but we're partners in every way. Equals. And I'm the luckiest woman alive.